THE MANUSCRIPT
MURDERS

THE MANUSCRIPT MURDERS

by

ROY HARLEY LEWIS

St. Martin's Press
New York

Author's Note
The characters in this book are my own and
bear no resemblance to any person living or
dead.

Library of Congress Cataloging in Publication Data

Lewis, Roy Harley.
The manuscript murders.

I. Title.
PR6062.E9543M35 1982   823'.914   81-21467
        ISBN 0-312-51391-7   AACR2

First published in Great Britain by Robert Hale Ltd.

ONE

After the rich promise of plushly carpeted corridors emerging from the show-cased foyer, the epitome of elegance, the large spartan room set aside for the sale of antiquarian books at the far end was no more imposing than a church hall. While no one would expect a tableau in champagne and mink by Cecil Beaton, surely to have anticipated a degree of *dignity*, a little *atmosphere*, does not make one an incurable romantic? Today was something special, after all, and while I was not exactly a newcomer to auction-rooms in London or the provinces, I had butterflies in my stomach at the prospect of bidding in £1,000's, as opposed to £10's, or even £100's. Nobody else seemed to care a damn.

Because of my relative inexperience of competing at this level, I had arrived early, too early, fearful of not getting a decent position. Now, with ten minutes to go, there were about sixty in the room, most of us interested in one, or at most half a dozen rare books in the sale catalogue — yet a stranger might have assumed we had very little in common. While I struggled to keep my excitement under control, to maintain a mask of mild interest, and to keep myself from getting up to stretch rebelliously stiff legs yet again, my rivals seemed intent on catching up on missed sleep, or chatting animatedly about subjects very remote from that which totally consumed my attention. On the surface it seemed that nobody in the room appreciated the importance of the occasion, yet I knew that as soon as the sale began nothing would escape their attention; and I, for all my single-mindedness, would be lucky to win, if 'win' was the right word. It worried me that to win, to secure lot 38, I might be forced to pay considerably over the odds, far more than the book was worth — although, again, who could say with authority what it was worth, other than what someone, individual or institution, was prepared to pay for it today.

Tom Duncan, librarian of the American university that I represented, had been frighteningly vague in his final telephone briefing.

"What's my ceiling price?" I had demanded.

Duncan had taken so long to reply that I wondered for a couple of moments whether our transatlantic connection had been severed, and then his words clarified nothing. "When it comes to the crunch, Matt, we'll have to rely on your judgement," he said, logically but confusing the issue, and then turned the screw with what appeared to be an afterthought. "We want it — but don't go mad."

I was tempted to replace the receiver, but in the midst of my frustration I remembered that I needed Duncan more than he needed me, or any individual bookseller. Biting back a sarcastic retort, I compromised by asking whether I had to submit a psychiatrist's report on the state of my mental health, along with the bill for my commission?

Duncan tried, despite the unbridled lust in his

6

tone, to be sympathetic to my problem. "Let me put it this way, Matt, I don't want to lose out to a toffee-nosed slob from the Ivy League universities. I'm sick and tired of getting egg on my face, trying to compete with bottomless money-bags, so this time I've broken open the piggy-bank, and we're putting the *works* on the Lanier nose. If there's some nutty private collector with money to burn, don't get involved, but if the stakes are high, but not crazy high, you just get in there pitching."

And yet, on reflection, Duncan's apparent vagueness was not out of character with the unmistakable aura of success he exuded. Anyone less like the conventional image of a librarian it is hard to imagine. Built like an athlete, and with the craggy facial features of a boxer — he had, in fact, been a Golden Gloves finalist in his youth — he was as tough as he looked. The fact that these days he fought tooth and nail over the acquisition of rare books made him a name to be respected on both sides of the Atlantic. It was this toughness and drive that had developed the college library until it ranked among the finest in the United States; and he would not be satisfied until it was the best.

I had already heard rumours of strenuous 'head-hunting' activities by at least three of the foremost universities; unfortunately for them it seemed that the substantial material wealth they dangled as bait meant little to Tom Duncan — not, at least, until he had achieved what he had set out to do.

A personal interest in Elizabethan, Jacobean and Restoration literature and theatre prompted his obsession with Emilia Lanier, the Dark Lady of Shakespeare's *Sonnets*. Although I had only met him once I sensed that the vagueness on the telephone was part of this obsessive personality, reflecting the single-mindedness that was concerned only with the end, undistracted by problems, anything he might dismiss as 'detail'.

I did not particularly like the rôle of agent at this level of international auction, because the small bookseller like myself is on to a hiding to nothing. I am obliged to invest time and to some extent money — in my case travel to London and overnight accommodation — and if my bid is not successful then I may earn nothing. Even if I am lucky, my obligation is to secure the book at the lowest possible price, which usually means that my 15% 'profit' on most small transactions is laughable. The problem is that, having been in the trade for such a short period, I needed all the contacts and commissions I could get. Duncan had only come to me because the bigger American universities were already represented at the major auctions by the old-established, so-called 'prestige' names in bookselling, and he and I had worked together once before. But even the Quaritchs, Maggs, and Frenshams of this world preferred to operate independently, especially when they already had a number of potential customers sometimes prepared to pay a considerably higher profit than an agent's commission.

As I surveyed the room for the umpteenth time, my nervousness increased; I was very much the amateur among the pros. It reminded me of a poker school, and the proverbial warning about playing with strangers. *They're not strangers*, I assured myself — at least not some of them. The fact that it was not my money at stake curiously seemed irrelevant. Would the *occasion* be too much for me? The test would be lot 38, although the catalogue entry, not counting the lengthy supplementary notes, appeared innocuous enough:

The property of Dr Hans van de Meeren
38. LANYER (AEmilia c 1569-1639) LATE 16TH CENTURY MANUSCRIPT JOURNAL. Fills 176 closely written (unnumbered) pages but imperfect at the beginning, and lacks two leaves (the third and the fifth) of the second gathering. Condition otherwise perfect. *Contemporary calf binding worn but intact.* Fcap (193 mm x 150 mm)

There were a number of reasons for the worldwide interest in the journal, but foremost was its coverage of certain significant periods (1590-93) in the life of Emilia Lanier who, only in recent years, had been identified as the Dark Lady of Shakespeare's *Sonnets.* In manuscript form, although quite handsomely bound in calf, the journal had been written as a diary, although the entries were irregular. Emilia had entrusted to the journal only what information she considered especially important, highlights and depressing periods in a relatively uneventful life as mistress to the Lord Chamberlain, Lord Hundsdon. It did, however, confirm in four separate matter-of-fact entries her relationship with Shakespeare, as well as other affairs which meant more to her, notably that with the Bard's friend and benefactor, the Earl of Southampton.

Until its discovery in Holland less than six months before, there was no evidence that the diary existed, and even now no indication why it had ended in Emilia's 24th year (forty years were to elapse before she died). As accomplished musician, in 1611 she was to write and publish a small book of poetry,

Salve Deus Rex Judaeorum, which places her at the forefront of women writers of her time. But the journal, written over a more interesting period, throws light not only on the Dark Lady but, although in small measure, England's greatest writer, and his times.

The manuscript had been kept in one Dutch family and seldom opened, probably because it was written in a foreign language, for about 350 years, which may explain why it was virtually still intact and in such good condition apart from the missing sheets and heavy dust staining. Dr van der Meeren, a university lecturer in business studies, was a direct descendant of a musician friend of the Laniers, who had presumably taken possession of the journals when Emilia died. Although the connection had long since been forgotten, and consequently with it the significance of the author's relationship with Shakespeare, he assumed from dates of the entries that it had some historical interest, if nothing else. Eventually, deciding to capitalise on his asset he consulted a colleague, the university librarian, who realised the journal was an exceptional find, and advised him to send it to London, where it was authenticated and its true potential value recognised.

With the dazed agreement of Dr van der Meeren, the reserve price was fixed at £30,000, although specialists at the auction house hoped it might fetch double that price, suggesting a catalogue guideline of £50,000. The estimate was based on the Shakespeare link, and to a lesser extent on the strong interest in female emancipation associated with Emilia's philosophy on life and sex expressed in her fêted book of poetry, published in 1611, two years after the publication of Shakespeare's *Sonnets*. But other

10

pointers were the sale in 1972 of an unknown play in manuscript (c 1611) by Shakespeare's contemporary, Thomas Heywood, for £45,000; and more remarkable, an old exercise book which belonged to the poet Robert Herrick (1591-1674), remembered for his lyrics to 'Cherry Ripe,' and containing 'Gather Ye Rose-buds while ye may . . .' which fetched £50,000.

My introspection was finally diverted by the appearance in the doorway of a young woman, the sort of blue-eyed, blonde bombshell that instinctively invites an indrawn whistle of admiration; not the distraction one normally associates with an auction room, although it must be said she turned practically every head in the room — on merit, and not on the novelty value. The newcomer was at first glance quite sensational, especially in the relatively austere setting, but on the closer examination she invited, there were minor flaws that made her more human, less like a screen goddess, and thus more attractive in my eyes. The profile, acquiline nose and sharply defined cheekbones was aristocratic, but mellowed by a sprinkling of freckles, while her mouth and lower jaw were too wide to match the perfection of the brow and eyes. A subconscious glance down revealed legs that were thicker than I generally like, but a small price to pay for the sum of the other attributes. The face and bearing indicated character and intelligence, and the full mouth contained that rare chemical equation that has never been properly defined, but is highly potent to any sexually impressionable man. She was, in fact, my type of woman and a welcome diversion from the strain of waiting for the auction to get under way.

She surveyed the room dispassionately, nodding

11

to several people with a half smile, but maintaining an enigmatic reserve. I thought at first she must have arrived with a very tall and emaciated, although otherwise rather ordinary individual, albeit somewhat sour-faced, who stood immediately behind her. But they did not speak to each other, and when she found a seat in the row in front of me he seemed to disappear — at least, I assumed that he sat somewhere at the back, although I was not sufficiently interested to look. Since she was only a few feet away I blessed my good fortune, anticipating an opportunity to catch her eye and open a conversation. In fact, I was still wallowing off-balance in a sea of ponderous clichés, when she looked my way. But as our eyes met, and held momentarily, I took a breath, and her gaze passed on.

Even as I cursed the missed opportunity, I was given a second chance by the arrival of Wilfred Frensham, the chairman of one of the country's oldest and most respected antiquarian booksellers, Frensham's of Grosvenor Square. Frensham, a former President of the Antiquarian Booksellers Association, and I moved in different worlds — he was very up-market by my standards — but we had developed a degree of mutual respect when, at his instigation, I had investigated a series of robberies of highly valuable rare books.* Rather to my surprise he made a bee-line towards me now, as cool and elegant as ever, reminding me more of a distinguished matinée idol than bookseller. In moments of soul-searching I had to admit to an element of envy at his success, his knowledge of antiquarian books, and, for a man in his late fifties, an obvious attrac-

* *A Cracking of Spines*

12

tion to women.

Despite my cynicism I could see that he was pleasantly surprised to see me; nor had his memory for names faltered in the six months since we had last met. "How is the delectable Laura?" he enquired with a twinkle after the more formal exchange.

People generally assumed that Laura Cottingham and I had an 'understanding', even though she lived and worked in London, and my bookshop was at Ardley in Dorset, about 150 miles to the West. The assumption was really a compliment to me, since Laura is an exceptionally attractive woman. But although we enjoyed a warm and very special intimacy, in the purely physical sense the relationship was inevitably affected by the geographical problem. The ball was in my court and I hedged uneasily, using the development of my new business as an excuse. Laura was a key executive with a leading advertising agency, and valued her independence; at least that was the impression she gave while I continued to hesitate over formalising the relationship. Frensham had been attracted to Laura but backed off like the gentleman he is when he realised the depth of her affection for me. He was, I had to concede, a totally unaffected and likeable man.

"Fine. She's just fine, thank you," I responded with a platitude that was even then only a half-truth, since I had not seen her for a couple of weeks. Rather typically, at the last moment when I realised I had to be in London for the auction, I phoned to see if Laura was free for dinner, but she had a prior engagement. My conscience would not allow me to accept her offer to break the date and mess her about any more than I had already. But I was too wary of Frensham to tell him the truth.

13

"Didn't expect to see you here today — what's the interest?" he enquired. I told him and he raised a respectful eyebrow. "Private customer, or institution?"

"Yes," I answered with deliberate vagueness. "What about you? I suppose it's not so very special by your standards?"

I had lost him; my question temporarily forgotten when he caught the eye of the blonde girl in front who had turned round at the sound of his voice. "Hello, Charlotte. How are you?" Remembering his manners he introduced us. "Matthew Coll — Charlotte Hesse, with an 'e'." He went on to give her a flattering picture of my shop in the country, although he could afford to be sincere, and then informed me that she worked as arts correspondent for one of the national newspapers. I realised then that I had seen the occasional byline, although I could not remember reading anything she had written.

"I couldn't help overhearing," she interrupted, as soon as the introductions were complete. "You're both going for the Lanier journal?" The husky voice was familiar, and I realised I had heard her broadcast from time to time in one of the BBC Radio arts programmes. The combination of sexy voice and the piercing blue eyes that appraised me made my heart skip a beat. As my brain strained to compute a suitably profound response that would impress, I had cause to bless the knack I had developed of maintaining a poker face, because in the event my little grey cells let me down, and I had to settle for what I hoped was an intriguing nod. But her eyes had long since transferred to Frensham.

Frensham gestured with a discreet finger to a

young man at the front — one of the countless number of apparently bored spectators who had, as a group, intimidated me at the outset. "That's Hugo Diringer, one of my directors. He's working. I'm only here from professional interest."

"But mainly the Lanier?" she enquired. Frensham nodded, "Then I hope you — " she turned apologetically to me — " or Mr Coll get it. It's too good a story to waste for it to be knocked down to an anonymous buyer. Nor is it just any rare book. I want to do an interview around Emilia Lanier."

Another incentive to win, I thought, as though one was needed. The appearance of the actioneer, Peter Ireland, prompted a fresh buzz of activity, and Frensham acknowledged us both before making his way to a seat that had obviously been kept for him by his fellow director, Diringer. Charlotte turned to the front, and in the ensuing moments I glanced instinctively for the last time at the supplementary notes in the catalogue beneath the Lanier lot entry, wondering inconsequentially how the author might have reacted to the fuss — and, more particularly, the respect her poetry had ultimately gained, albeit 350 years too late. The passage had been practically committed to memory:

. . . Most Elizabethan scholars now accept the A L Rowse theory that Emilia Lanier was the Dark Lady of Shakespeare's *Sonnets*. Born in 1569, daughter of Baptista Bassano, a musician from Venice who had settled in London and married an English-woman, Emilia at eighteen was left alone, to fend for herself. She became mistress to Lord Hunsdon, the Lord Chamberlain, being kept by him for several years before being obliged to marry Alfonso Lanier for the sake of convenience, when she gave birth to Hunsdon's son. By this time Hunsdon had his own company of actors, which is probably how she met Shakespeare and became the object of his passions. Scholars who have long since praised the quality of her poetry in *Salve Deus Rex Judaeorum*, which appeared two years after the publication of the *Sonnets*, have welcomed the journal's discovery. It is expected, after further detailed study, to throw considerable light on English society at the end of the 16th century, as well as providing the long-awaited evidence of Emilia's affaire with Shakespeare . . .

There followed a dozen or so very short extracts spanning the years covered by the journal, with an additional note explaining that the script fluctuates slightly in size and style, which (taking into account the use of different pens) was a possible reflection of the writer's different moods as her circumstances changed.

When I looked up, Peter Ireland was racing through the early lots, and my hands began to perspire at the prospect of the coming ordeal. Despite the large sums of money involved, I knew that it would be over in a matter of minutes, that I would not have time to deliberate, and would have to react instinctively in the thick of the skirmish. With the auction house's own estimate of £50,000 being (although only a guideline) a realistic one, I had thought long and hard about the merits of deciding on a ceiling price and sticking to it, but there were so many imponderables that it was impractical to stick to a plan. In the end, as Tom

Duncan had suggested, it would be a gut reaction. I would *know*.

"Lot 38, the journal of Emilia Lanier," Ireland droned in his phlegmatic manner, "written in her own hand . . ." Without further preamble he looked up and announced, "I must say £12,000 to start."

That was an indication that he had received a written bid for that amount. I waited to see what would happen and watched his eyes scan the room. "Thirteen thousand, fourteen, fifteen, sixteen, seventeen, eighteen, nineteen, twenty . . ." The sum climbed with frightening speed, and I marvelled at his ability to encompass the birds from so many directions, when I could barely make out any positive movement. He had reached £40,000 in thirty seconds, and there was a pause while the bidders seemed to get their second wind. I raised a finger and he looked at me, acknowledging the bid. "Forty-one thousand." Then they were off again, although from the direction of Ireland's gaze, I assumed that the number of people still in the hunt had been cut to about four — five, including me. There was another, longer pause at £50,000, so I raised another finger. Acknowledging my bid, this time he scanned the room more carefully, coming to rest at Hugo Diringer. "Fifty-three thousand." Someone, unseen, behind and to the other side of me raised the bidding to fifty-five thousand. Again I held up three fingers, only to be capped by Diringer.

The price was now standing at £60,000, and there were only three of us still in contention. Frensham's firm would take some beating if they were really determined; they could afford to buy the book for stock, knowing they had some of the world's richest collectors among their customers, and if they were

17

representing an institutional library the chances were that it was much larger and much richer than my client. My hope, however, was that Diringer might have marked anything up to a dozen items, less newsworthy than the Lanier but probably more profitable in resale terms. While I hesitated, the unknown person behind me raised the bid by another £3,000. I glanced at Diringer, and his expression was strained. He had obviously reached his limit and was undecided whether to go over the top. Next to him, Frensham's face was serene; he had been through this experience many times before, and was content to back his colleague's judgement, even if it meant the younger man losing this time but learning from experience. Ireland looked at me, and the gavel in his hand started to rise. My own nerves had disappeared and I felt as thought I were playing poker. Almost without thinking I took a calculated gamble, and raised five fingers. "Sixty-eight thousand pounds," acknowledged Ireland. He looked back to the unidentified man behind me, and then at Diringer — and drew no reaction. "Sixty-eight thousand pounds," he repeated. I waited with bated breath for him to announce it for a third time, but he knew instinctively that the others had conceded, and down came his hammer. It was mine.

I was overjoyed yet stunned, not knowing whether to stand up and take a bow or to be terribly blasé — but if I was overwhelmed, very few others even bothered to look my way. Ireland had started on the next lot before it registered that among the visible reactions had been a genuinely delighted smile from Frensham, and a more restrained but equally sincere whispered congratulation from Charlotte Hesse, who then turned back to scribble something

18

in her notebook.

In the state of mild euphoria, my next thought was for Tom Duncan and his reaction to the news. Looking back, I can say hand-on-heart that the commission I had just earned did not even occur to me. It was nearly lunch-time but just after 5 a.m on Tom's side of the Atlantic, and although I would not have hesitated to wake him, I only had the college telephone number, so that call would have to wait. The next few minutes were rather an anti-climax, the sensation of surfing inshore on a giant wave and being left high and dry excited still yet uncomfortably restrained. I wanted to jump on my seat, interrupt the proceedings and demand attention, but I guessed that no one else would have appreciated the gesture.

However, I was obviously on a winning streak, and fate decided my next course of action when Charlotte Hesse turned and beckoned with a finger. "If you're not bidding for anything else," she whispered, "can I get that interview?" I had to lean forward to catch the words, and her blue eyes in close-up lifted my spirits still higher. I looked at my wrist-watch pointedly. "Over lunch, if you like?"

She nodded and made her way to the exit, while I went through the formalities of confirming my purchase, in the knowledge that the funds would be telexed within a matter of hours. I would call back later that afternoon.

It was perhaps an indication of her striking appearance that on joining her outside I noticed the portable tape-recorder for the first time, and possibly then only because she drew attention to it in her opening remarks.

"We can use one of the empty offices upstairs,"

19

she said. "I've already got some background atmosphere."

I shrugged my willingness to fall in with her technical priorities, and followed her up a single flight of stairs to an office she had presumably used before from the way she walked in, without a knock, or even a preliminary glance inside.

We sat down at a desk, and while preparing the recorder she ran through the questions she intended to put, very professional, and relevant to the subject — none, thank goodness, of the excruciating "You must feel very pleased to have won . . ." variety. Indeed, not only was she familiar with antiquarian books and their values, but certainly far more knowledgeable than me about Emilia Lanier and her background, although I was able to finesse grey areas with reference to Tom Duncan's expertise on the 16th and 17th centuries. When it was over I looked at my watch and saw that we had been recording for 20 minutes, although she was quick to point out that the tape would be edited to little more than five. "I shall also write something for the paper — try to deal with separate issues," she added.

"Where shall we eat?" I asked. "I'm a little out of touch, living in the wilds."

She glanced at her watch and pouted slightly. "Oh — I didn't realise how late it was," she said, looking at me with an expression of disappointment that I could only hope was genuine. "Would you mind if we skipped a meal this time?"

I did mind, and said so, pointing out that the interview had been conditional on lunch. "I hate eating on my own, especially among all these City slickers."

She smiled. "If it's protection you want, I suppose

20

it's the least I can do. A pub lunch is quick — there's the 'Mason's Arms' just out back."

Still uplifted by my recent success, I would have preferred a traditional celebration topped with champagne, but it was her company that came first, and a glance at some of the familiar faces at the bar — among them the most distinguished names in the antiquarian book trade — brought me down to earth. Men who were accustomed to paying anything up to ten times the figure I had successfully bid that morning, often with their *own* money, and returning to hot sausages on sticks and pints of draught beer, would not accept me as one of them until I learned to win, and lose, with equanimity. Characteristically unpretentious, Charlotte also seemed happy with beer and sandwiches. Come to think of it, the English public house, packed to capacity at lunch-time, is a great social class leveller; it is impossible to stand on one's dignity while jostled from every angle. However, we managed to find a reasonably safe window-seat where we were able to eat and talk in relative privacy, fenced in by the bodies and legs of those having to stand.

I intended to see more of Charlotte Hesse, and made no effort to disguise my interest, but trying to penetrate her reserve was an uphill struggle. She was pleasant enough superficially, yet held back, seeming to manipulate my questions so that most of the conversation was about myself, elaborating on what Frensham had told her. I was not in the habit of talking about myself, but I had to do something to gain her confidence, so I explained the way I had opted out of the rat race (I had been personal assistant in a trouble-shooting capacity to the Chairman of one of the biggest newspaper groups in Fleet

Street) to buy the delightful bookshop I now ran in Dorset. Of course, my enthusiasm got the better of my discretion, and I rambled on to the threshold of boredom about my old Queen Anne house with its converted shop facing on to the High Street. The shop, bursting at the seams with charm and atmosphere, is featured in a number of tourist guides, and I can talk about it proudly yet without embarrassment because the credit is not really mine. The picture I have painted is the life's work of my predecessor, and I had merely taken over on his retirement, constantly adding to the stock, of course, and trying to inject just a little of my own personality.

A beautiful old house and shop to match I've found is a useful subject for attracting friends, particularly of the opposite sex, as though some of that character and interest rubs off on you; rather like taking the dog for a walk. Laura Cottingham, for example, was captivated by the place. Charlotte seemed to find it all very interesting, yet when I invited her to Ardley to see for herself, her smile was somewhat mechanical, and I sensed that she would not take up the offer. At this point I decided to cut my losses. Apart from Laura, I was never short of attractive women friends and had no intention of forcing my attentions where they were clearly not welcome. Yet strangely, as soon as I made that clear, she seemed to relax and became more forthright in her answers.

She was *not*, she insisted with patient resignation, related to Herman Hesse the author, although her great-grandfather had come from Germany. She had studied art and literature and now used that knowledge in her journalism. Her parents were still alive and lived in North Wales; otherwise she was independent and had no ties. Statements of fact, yet somehow still giving little away. My initial mild infatuation dissipated, I warmed to her directness and respected her reserve. Clearly she was not easy, despite her looks, in relationships; something was missing. Something more than the occasional smile, for example, let alone laugh, would have been welcome, yet while she responded in a limited way to my sense of humour, not once did she attempt to lighten the conversation. Laura's personality, in contrast, is so engaging as to be positively intimidating at times. Significantly, Frensham had remembered her, while he did not seem to have been over-impressed with Charlotte. Beginning to see her more in perspective, I wondered what she would find to talk about outside a 'business' environment. But there was obviously more in her than meets the eye, and I realised that given the time and opportunity I could get beneath that impersonal veneer — that, in those circumstances, she could still excite me.

However, tired of forcing the pace, I decided it was time to leave, and glanced casually at the throng, just beginning to thin out. My eyes caught those of a tall, gangling man in his early forties. Apart from his height, there was little to distinguish him, thinning hair, pale, even features — yet his face seemed familiar. We stared at each other dispassionately for a second, and I remembered I had seen him arrive at the auction at the same time as Charlotte. I turned back to my companion. "Are you going back to the office now?" I enquired, conscious of mouthing platitudes.

She nodded, gathering up her recorder. Before getting to my feet something made me look over my shoulder again. The tall man was staring at Charlotte

23

this time, so intently that he was oblivious of my obvious curiosity. I drew her attention to him. "Don't look now," I said dramatically, but with a hint of a smile, "you have a very passionate-looking admirer over to my left. Do you know him by any chance?"

Her eyes followed the imperceptible movement of my head, and dismissed him, returning to her recorder and handbag. "No", she added, almost as an afterthought.

"I noticed him arriving at the sale. He was just behind you, and for a moment I assumed you were together."

"I'll get a taxi," she said, closing the subject.

I followed her outside into Hanover Square. "It's been nice," I said. "I'm in the phone book if you are ever in the West Country. Meanwhile, I presume I can reach you through the paper?"

She nodded and simultaneously hailed a taxi that had just entered the Square. As it drew up alongside, she extended her hand in a businesslike manner, and thanked me for the interview with a smile — more than polite, but only barely scratching at the surface of friendship. Then she was gone.

I reflected on the events of the past few hours. The main feature was that I had secured the Lanier for Tom Duncan, and my immediate priority was to telephone him. I gave a mental shrug at the thought of the departing Charlotte. You can't win them all. I turned on my heel and was momentarily disconcerted to see the tall man from the pub looking in my direction from the corner of Maddox Street. When I returned his stare, his eyes seemed to glaze over, and he walked away.

Surely he had not followed me? Charlottte perhaps?

I dismissed them both from my thoughts. I had work to do.

TWO

The remainder of that memorable day was spent contentedly handling and browsing through the manuscript, increasingly conscious of the fact that it would soon be lost to me. Running my fingers featherlike over the precariously thin pages, almost sensing the private thought of Emilia Lanier, in some ways like a blind man reading braille, was an awe-inspiring experience; the ink, startlingly black (although perhaps no so surprising since the journal had seldom been opened, and it is light which causes fading), seemed to demand attention as though endowed with the power of Emilia's personality. It was a sensation of the utmost intimacy, as though she had written for my eyes alone, especially as with only the slightest stretch of the imagination the diary might have been mine.

The underlying impression was that I was meeting a person still very much alive, fallible, at times unreasonable and even bloody-minded, but intelligent and basically warm-hearted — not the necessarily one-sided view presented by a tortured Shakespeare; and I was conscious of a danger that if I read much more I would become obsessed with the woman. Her words represented to me a priceless treasure of human emotion, but there were other little clues to her personality. Not only did the handwriting vary according to her mood, or the pen she used, but there were what I took for other indirect signs of agitation or frustration, such as a reverse print of her writing on the back of the previous page where the journal had been closed hurriedly before the ink was dry. This had happened on a number of occasions, and each time the entry had revealed cause for complaint or even distress.

In the weeks that followed I was brought down to earth by the routine activities involved in running a bookshop. Although my unexpected success had whetted my appetite for the big auction, I knew that — apart from receiving other commissions — I was not yet ready for buying and selling at that level on my own account. I had developed a healthy mail order catalogue trade to boost earnings over the counter, but my more expensive books generally sold for under £100, with the occasional collectors' item fetching perhaps a few hundred. Yet men like Frensham regarded the Lanier journal in much the same context, multiplied many times over. They could afford to back their judgement in a matter of tens of thousand of pounds — and wait, if necessary, until they had found an appreciative customer at the right price. However, I had no regrets.

Some of my friends had wondered why, in my early thirties, I had wanted to leave London where 'it's all happening'. Well, perhaps my view was somewhat jaundiced, but I no longer much liked what I saw there. I had come to Ardley, inspired by my love of old books, and enthused not only by the shop but by an environment of timeless beauty, and had no intention of spending half my life sitting in draughty auction rooms, especially in London. Mind you, whenever friends visited my rambling six-bedroomed Queen Anne house and looked out of an upstairs back window over the sweeping panorama of Dorset hills — they became curiously envious, as though I had not been completely honest; had been holding out on them. The house had been built in 1723 on the brow of a hill, so that on a clear day one could see almost sixty miles of coastline.

Two ground-floor rooms at the front, facing the village High Street, had been converted into the shop which was itself a browser's dream. An imposing open-beamed fireplace restored by my predecessor, with bookshelves on either side, and a pair of long-handled copper bed-warmers above, had to compete for attention in a setting that was full of attractive features — assorted hunting-horns, antique guns and swords dotted about, among nearly 20,000 second-hand and antiquarian books. Even Wilfred Frensham, who must have been everywhere and seen everything in his years in the trade, had been stopped in his tracks.

Yet although I was basically happy, and too busy to brood over the excitement of the 'big time', there were occasional twinges, especially when I had to contend with some of the headaches of shop life — the kids with fingers sticky from ice lollies or chocolate bars who had to be endured because they *might* grow up to become bibliophiles; the browsers who practically turned out the whole stock and left without buying even a paperback; weird characters who treated the place like a free lending library; and even the occasional drunk from the pub next door who wanted the current copy of *Sporting Life*,

28

and became aggressive when told we did not stock it. Possible violence was the least of my worries; I might have welcomed the exercise. I managed to keep fit by running three or four miles every morning before breakfast, and persevering with my Canadian Air Force exercises, but from time to time I wished there was a proper gymnasium on my doorstep, or the opportunity to engage in more explosive forms of exercise.

Five weeks after the Lanier sale, I was stunned to read a small paragraph on the front page of *The Times*:

Amsterdam. Thursday.
The good fortune that led university professor, Dr H. van de Meeren, to a rare English manuscript in his attic — and the £68,000 it fetched at the recent London auction, deserted him today. The professor was found dead at his home from head injuries after apparently disturbing burglars. A police spokesman confirmed that the attack was being treated as a murder investigation.

I read the paragraph a dozen times or more, trying to make sense of it. Although van der Meeren had not come to London for the auction, and I had not met him, I felt a sense of loss, if only from the interest we had shared for a short period, no doubt with the same intensity. The report was frustratingly uninformative, although I realised that the death of a foreign national, several hundred miles away, was of little interest to the British press. At least one fact was in correct — the journal had not been found in an attic, but that was unimportant. How tragic that he should be killed — and in such frightening circumstances — only a month or so after coming into what was for him a small fortune? An inconsequential thought flashed through my mind — *Perhaps the diary had a curse on it*? Perhaps the title 'Dark Lady' had an entirely different connotation; which meant that the thief, or thieves, might also not live to enjoy the money they had presumably taken. I pushed the wild idea aside impatiently, and my thoughts returned to the unfortunate van der Meeren. Sudden wealth had often brought with it misfortune, as pools or lottery winners had discovered to their cost, but never murder.

I had a living to earn, but for the next few days the murdered man was never far from my thoughts, as though there was a psychic link between us, vender and buyer, established by the medium we shared — Emilia Lanier. I had to know more about the murder, and eventually I did something positive about it — phoning an old colleague on the *Daily Chronicle*, George Kester, its successful columnist. Kester promised to get back when he had collected the reports, obviously sniffing a story, but I was too preoccupied to elaborate on my interest. I felt strangely uneasy. Should I contact Tom Duncan?

Why? I answered myself irritably. *What has it got to do with him?*

Nothing, but he might want to know . . .

I tried to shake off the train of thought, pacing up and down and glancing from time to time at the bookshelves, as though for inspiration. One title seemed to leap out, at me — or perhaps it was merely the shiny dust jacket — *The Solemn Mockery*, which I remembered was a historical account of famous book and manuscript forgeries. My nerve-ends started to fray. You're developing a persecution complex, I warned myself. But in such an apprehensive frame of mind even the wildest assumptions suddenly appear quite reasonable. What did I know about 16th-century mss? I pulled myself together. The journal had been examined by those who *did*. The auction room had no doubt, and nor did most of the important dealers — including Frensham, possibly respected more than anyone. If the worst came to the worst Tom Duncan could not blame me. In any case, he and his colleagues had been closetted with the journal for not far short of a month; coming from abroad there had been no problem over an export licence which sometimes happens with rare works, when the 'prior' claims of the nation are suddenly raised.

I had recovered my composure by the time Kester returned my call. The news was disappointing. Kester had collated two rival agency reports, and a routine check from the paper's correspondent in Amsterdam, but there was little fresh information. The house had been ransacked, and there were signs of a struggle when Dr van der Meeren had apparently disturbed the intruders. He had been beaten about the head and shoulders with a heavy silver candle-stick.

"What about the money?" I asked. "It couldn't have been a run-of-the-mill break-in out of the blue?"

He was quiet for a few seconds, presumably re-reading the reports. "There's no mention of it here. Obviously the police are not saying too much."

He was probably right, which only added to my frustration. I thought of the unfortunate doctor, and echoed my thoughts: "Poor sod."

Kester grunted sympathetically. "Terrible thing. Anything we can quote you on?"

"You must be joking." His hypocrisy irritated

31

me, although I realised he was merely doing his job.

"Well, *something*, anything," he added unabashed. "You're the only lead we have."

"The story would have gone on the spike if I hadn't telephoned," I pointed out. "Do me a favour, George, kill it. I've got a purely personal interest in the guy, and if it produces anything I'll let you know."

When I had replaced the receiver, I cursed myself for sounding more dramatic than I had intended. What on earth could I produce? Just the same, I had an unsettling sense of involvement, as though I owed van der Meeren something; illogical, but a gut reaction.

I suddenly felt I had to get away for a few days. Whether my restlessness was fired by that desire, or more by what I mentioned before in passing — about the chores — it is difficult to recall, but either was probably as good an excuse as any for going on a book-buying trip. Normally it was not practical to travel beyond a 100-miles radius in the never-ending search for new stock, and since taking over the shop, going abroad for the purpose had not even entered my mind.

Now Holland suddenly seemed an attractive proposition; there were at least a couple of anti-quarian booksellers I had heard of in Amsterdam, as well as others in The Hague and Rotterdam, all within striking distance by car or train, once I was there. I could afford to invest some of the income from the Lanier sale in the sort of better-than-usual stock I might find in what was to me virgin territory. And while I was out there, I could surely spare *five* or ten minutes to speak to the police investigating van der Meeren's death . . .

I telephoned Charlie Appleton, a retired bookseller Frensham had recommended when the Antiquarian Booksellers Association had called on my services as an investigator*, and who had proved a tremendous asset to the business, as well as becoming a good friend. On that occasion, Frensham had paid for Charlie's time, but now I was reasonably independent I did not hesitate to see if he could look after the shop for a few days. Charlie is the sort of man who would have come for nothing, but we concluded a businesslike arrangement, and then I felt free to contact the travel agent I knew in Lyme Regis.

Over the years I had travelled fairly extensively, and although I am still romantic enough to rubber-neck like the stereotype tourist, I've come to the conclusion that the differences one expects from different countries are disappearing at an alarming rate. The old gag about American tourists taking in Europe, "It must be Tuesday, this is Italy", is no longer funny because so many countries and cities increasingly look alike. Airports, for example, all look the same; so do the motorways from airport to city centres; and the newer hotels are identical. Amsterdam has much of this reassuring (for those who feel they need it) sameness, coupled with a feature that is unique — the canals. I am not unaware of Venice's claims, but the balance of water to land is such that the atmosphere is totally different. Amsterdam is also cleaner and does not smell quite so much — sweeping statements, perhaps, but I can only speak as I find, and I like Amsterdam. I also like the Dutch.

I got a taxi to the green and smoke-glass skyscraper that could only have been a hotel, and began ringing round to make appointments; far less of a hassle

* *A Cracking of Spines*

there than in any other European city because practically everyone seems to speak flawless English. I began with the police, as it happens, persuading myself that by getting van der Meeren out of my hair I could concentrate more easily on book buying. I was lucky, starting logically with the Central Reserche bureau, and finding my investigating team on the third extensio⟩, without the bureaucratic fuss one usually associates with police departments the world over, and I was promised an appointment with an Inspector James Heemskerk at 10 a.m. next morning.

Frensham had given me a personal introduction to the old-established booksellers, Van der Bogaarde, in the Purmerendstraat, and I spent a profitable afternoon looking through their stock of English language books in a variety of subjects, the size of which was only a mild surprise in view of the interest the Dutch have in all things English; the Netherlands must be the only country in the world where daily newspapers bother to review foreign (in their case, English) books. There were no bargains in the conventional sense of the word, but one of the real headaches of my trade is actually replacing decent books that have been sold, so I was happy to pick up a dozen or so early 19th-century travel-books with the engravings that make them so attractive, for a reasonable price, although £250 represented more than half my budget in one fell swoop. Most of the modern first editions were too expensive for buying 'on spec', but my investment in the travel-books was rewarded when a delighted assistant escorted me to the basement and produced a number of boxes of thrillers and general fiction, and what might be described as 'shelf-fillers', which he complained were taking up too much room. I was made to feel almost philanthropic in taking them off their hands for a nominal sum, and the potential profit margin in that bargain lot was enough to cover most of my expenses while in the city.

Henk van der Bogaarde, grandson of the firm's founder, and a friendly if somewhat supercilious individual, insisted on taking me to dinner at my hotel, which seemed a strange choice for someone who should have known where to find better 'local' *haut cuisine*, but perhaps he enjoyed slumming occasionally, and I suppose I did not rate an invitation to his home. For a big man, his voice was surprisingly high. The accent was heavy, although the vocabularly was as comprehensive as one comes to expect, and the time passed pleasantly enough, so I took the opportunity to ask if there had been any gossip in the trade about the ill-fated van der Meeren. He laughed, and remembering my association, shrugged and added rather more discreetly: "You know how people try to read between the lines."

"I understood the evidence was straight forward?"

"What I think you would call 'circumstantial' evidence can be *too* straight forward."

"Implying what?"

"Pardon?"

"Implying that it was not a simple murder during a robbery?"

He nodded briskly; a fat man, his double chin seemed to vibrate in unison with the movement of his head. "I do not believe that myself, you understand, but people are asking why the police are so silent about the money — keeping the cards, as you say, close to their chests."

Which is surely routine procedure, I thought. It's not the job of the police to speculate like — booksellers. I asked what the message 'between the lines' revealed to those apparently better informed.

He did not know whether or not I was being sarcastic, but the reply was considered and solemn enough. "The suggestion is that the late van der Meeren was not as pure as he pretended."

Despite my contempt for uninformed conjecture my heart sank. "You are suggesting that he was involved in a fraud of some sort — and subsequently quarrelled with his partners in crime?"

"Not I, my friend. Although I have to admit the theory comes from men not usually given to fantasy."

"But what evidence is there for this theory?" I protested.

He shrugged. "None, of course. But you have to remember that in this country the experts are very sensitive. Art dealers have been made to look very foolish on a number of occasions, and some of my colleagues in the book trade are anxious that they should be seen as too shrewd to be taken-in. It is human nature to be wise after the event, or if one is not involved, but if *they* had examined the manuscript . . ." He shrugged again without bothering to finish the sentence.

Despite my better judgement I felt stupidly defensive over my own lack of expertise in manuscripts, but I managed to conceal the irritation. I had little doubt that my host was just as 'wise' as the colleagues he now patronised. "All I can add," I remarked, with an edge to my voice, "is that having read some of the entries I find it hard to accept that anyone today could get into the mind of Emilia Lanier to the extent of fabricating what has been written. It is a work of considerable literary merit."

He nodded sympathetically. "Certainly not in this country, for all our familiarity with the language. The dead man's subject was business studies, and from what I hear he made no pretence of knowing anything about English history. There is, of course, the other possibility that the *manuscript* is perfectly genuine, but that van der Meeren stole it from the true owner."

I told him about my appointment next morning, and he looked surprised. "Forgive me, Matthew, but I do not see what you can hope to achieve? You are satisfied that the manuscript is authentic, so why confuse the issue by investigating irrelevancies? If people get to hear of it they will jump to the wrong conclusions, and you will make life difficult for yourself. A man is presumed innocent until he is proved guilty, and by the same token the onus is on the doubters to prove their case, not for you to justify its legitimacy."

He was probably just trying to be loyal, one bookseller to another, not really very interested in the truth about the manuscript. "It is not something I can explain," I replied, not knowing why I bothered. "I feel almost an obligation, as though Emilia Lanier had brought us together. If I was really worried about a forgery all I have to do is to contact the new owners and suggest that they run a couple of laboratory tests, which would settle the issue once and for all."

"Exactly," he said emphatically. "But it is a matter for them, not you."

The sentiment was very much to the forefront of my mind when I entered the office of Inspector

Heemskerk next day. He was a fair and balding man in his middle forties, athletically built and exuding a composure that was calculated to reassure the public at large, and unsettle the criminal. I guessed from the spaciousness of the room, and the quality of the furniture and accessories, that he would not remain as Inspector for very long. His English was impeccable, with almost no trace of an accent — an accomplishment he played down in his opening remarks by explaining that his mother was English. But I doubted whether that had anything to do with it; one could tell from the way he moved, the way he dressed, and his general manner that he was the sort of person who did everything well.

It was perhaps significant that in the preliminary pleasantries Heemskerk offered me a *choice* of tea or coffee. I was impressed. The man was obviously a high flyer. Over the coffee I had chosen with rather typical English conservatism — doubting the foreigner's ability to make tea properly — we covered much of the ground explored with van der Bogaarde, although I did not mention the theories of those who considered themselves brighter than the police. Throughout, Heemskerk wore the same expression of benign concern, a reminder to anyone who cared what a nice and helpful bunch the Amsterdam police were.

Eventually, the coffee gone and my patience beginning to wear a little thin, I asked if he had any leads.

He smiled reassuringly. "Our enquiries are proceeding satisfactorily. In a murder enquiry there is a considerable amount of detailed work that is very time-consuming."

"Of course, but there must have been clues. Were

the intruders professionals?"

He replied with another question. "How much would you have expected the late Dr van der Meeren to have received from the sale of the manuscripts?"

I was momentarily confused. "You can work it out yourself from the sale price. The only outgoing was the commission charged by the auction house, which is standard, and a very small amount for expenses — I should say . . ."

He stopped me with a shake of the head. "The exact amount is not important, Mr Coll. But using round figures for the sake of convenience, if that total was £50,000, you would have expected him to put it in the bank?" His raised eyebrows posed the question.

"He didn't?" I demanded fatuously.

"His bank account is in credit to the sum of well, the equivalent of just under £2,000 in sterling. Most of that was deposited about six months ago, and since then nothing of any consequence has gone in or out. Now Mr Coll, why should a man who has entrusted his modest savings to the same bank for over twenty years suddenly break the habit of a life-time? We are not dealing with a peasant who suddenly wins a fortune in a sweepstake and does not know how to cope — anyone with a grain of sense would surely realise he was *inviting* trouble."

"What about currency restrictions, or possible tax evasion? Perhaps it all went to an unnumbered Swiss bank account?"

He shook his head. "Van der Meeren's good fortune was too well documented; nor did he have anything to fear from the authorities. If he had a secret fetish about counting the money every night before going to sleep, he would have needed an accessible hiding-place — something a little less obvious than the mattress, or under the carpet — which presents something of a problem. Even with large denomination bank-notes it would have made a bulky package, and it is not easy to hide that sort of thing from a determined thief. Someone ransacked the house thoroughly — *every* drawer and *every* crack and crevice — turned the place upside down . . ."

"And . . ."

He seemed surprised at my bland acceptance of the information.

"Let us assume that we are dealing with professionals, and ask yourself: would such men systematically start from the logical beginning, and then cover every centimetre square by square? It would take them hours or even days. Surely, men ruthless enough to kill if disturbed, rather than make their escape, would also save themselves all that time and effort by forcing their victim to reveal his hiding-place."

I agreed. "Certainly more efficient than creeping about in the dark with a torch — unless he surprised them, and they panicked."

He shook his head, without bothering to explain his reasons, and continued: "Any reasonable man would have given them the information they needed without resort to torture. And since you mention efficiency — there is another consideration. I find it hard to believe that men efficient enough to wear gloves — and there are no finger-prints on the murder weapon, or indeed anything — would not have left such chaos. From my experience, mess is the hall-mark of amateurs."

"Then perhaps they were."

He shook his head again confidently. "According to the housekeeper — *nothing* was taken, apart from money that she would not have known about. There were several expensive ornaments, pieces of silver and *objet d'art* which would have been an irresistible temptation. In my view, two possibilities emerge. First, which seems less likely, they lost their nerves after killing him and ran. Second: the chaos was created for our benefit . . ."

"To make you think in terms of a burglary? The suggestion behind that theory is that he was killed for a different reason."

Heemskerk smiled. "You are jumping ahead too quickly. Think back to the money; forget motive at this stage. Where is it? *Not* the bank, the most likely place, and not in the house. If it was *not* stolen, did it really exist?"

I was confused. "We know there was a banker's draft which he, assuming it was him, cashed."

"But what we do not know is whether that money was his by right? Or did it have to be shared out with other persons, as yet unknown . . ."

My heart sank. " . . . who might have been involved in a conspiracy, which in turn points to a forgery?"

"Who knows anything?" he responded with a shrug. He stared at me dispassionately, the benign mask forsaken for a moment or two, before deciding to put his cards on the table. "A man of your background, Mr Coll, would surely not take offence if I admitted quite frankly that for a brief moment I even had my doubts about you. If there was a conspiracy, would it not be useful to have a confederate at the auction, either to raise the price artificially, or merely to establish the authenticity of such a forgery on the open market for all to see?"

41

"Expensive way of proving the point — paying £68,000 for one's own forgery," I commented.

"Come now, Mr Coll, as a bookseller you must agree that if one was less concerned with the profit element, he could recoup his money practically overnight. That manuscript has gained a pedigree and with world-wide inflation it must already be worth more than £68,000."

I conceded the point, and queried his other assumption. "Why should you be concerned with my sensitivity?"

"One of my first reactions was to run a routine check just to make sure you were a genuine bookseller. Then, after your call yesterday, I telexed a request for further background information from my friends at Scotland Yard. They were able to produce an Inspector at your local CID who knows you, and from him we discovered that you were once on our side of the fence."

"*Military* intelligence," I corrected mildly. "Did that mean I was automatically classified as innocent?"

He grinned. "It means you might be in a position to help me. There are no grounds to justify an official approach to the British police, merely my —" he hesitated, searching for the word in English — "my intuition."

"It all *sounds* reasonable," I conceded. "But there is also a distinct possibility that your analysis is over-sophisticated. We could just be dealing with petty crooks who panicked and did everything wrong. It's a basic premise you can't afford to ignore."

"We ignore nothing, but I did not attain my present rank by simply accepting information on its face value."

He seemed unconcerned, but I sensed I had touched

42

a sensitive area — Heemskerk, the smooth professional, liked to be given credit for imagination, as well as intelligence. I could not resist ruffling his feathers a little more. "During the war, German Intelligence intercepted a top-secret Allied communiqué that Stalin, Churchill and Roosevelt were proposing to attend a summit meeting at Casablanca. They thought the message was a trick, and that the location was too obvious to be genuine, and chose to interpret Casablanca as the White House . . . They were wrong."

Heemskerk shrugged. "We will see."

Having made my point, I set out to restore our apparent rapport. "Like you, I believe in following my intuition. Obviously the authenticity of the manuscript becomes a crucial issue. I shall contact Tom Duncan and suggest — and that is all I can do — that they get the paper and ink analysed. No fake, no matter how cleverly produced, can get by the various laboratory tests."

"If these tests are so foolproof, why are they not applied automatically whenever something of this age suddenly appears from out of the blue?"

I shrugged. "Forgeries are very rare because it can seldom be worth the enormous bother — the painstaking effort to match paper and type-faces — in relation to the *risks* involved. It would be much easier to steal a Gutenberg bible, for example, than attempt to copy it to the standard required. And if something of that calibre was to turn up in — say — the bricked-in vault of a 15th-century German church, then the book world would still be extremely suspicious and insist on satisfying itself by scientific means. But they have to draw the line somewhere."

"Is it not more likely that scholars and biblio-philes *want* to believe the object as genuine?" he interjected with a note of cynicism, obviously getting back at me for my criticism a few moments earlier. "They subconsciously meet the forger half-way."

"Perhaps."

"And have you altered your opinion about the manuscript?"

I smiled and shrugged. "I am an optimist, so I must remain hopeful, but meanwhile it would be sensible to assume the worst. If my bookseller friend was correct in his theory that a forgery was beyond Dr van der Meeren, one would have to look elsewhere, probably to England. Did the professor have any known contacts abroad?"

"We have drawn a blank so far."

"Nothing at his home to give a clue?"

"You are welcome to take a look, Mr Coll, but take my word for it, you would be wasting your time. He lived just off the Zwanveld about ten minutes' drive from here; a fairly typical area for the professional classes, picture windows, green wooden shutters, pretty but rather characterless. We have been through the place from top to bottom — nothing."

"Did his housekeeper live in?"

"Unfortunately not. She would only know if he had visitors from the evidence of unwashed glasses or cigarette stubs, since he did not smoke — or drink much. Neighbours have seen occasional visitors, but not the sort of people they might reasonably recognise later, and certainly nothing to indicate nationality."

"I understand, but would it be possible to see those reports? In certain circumstances I might recognise an English person from the way he dressed — from some small idiosyncrasy that you, as a Dutchman, might not appreciate."

He nodded. "I shall have photostats sent round to your hotel." He stood up. "Please keep in touch, Mr Coll, and let me know what transpires from your call to the United States."

I left feeling depressed, and not even the rest of the day book hunting could shake off my fear that the Lanier was a forgery. Yet I could not bring myself to shatter Tom Duncan's world on such flimsy evidence, convincing myself that another day or two would hardly matter. When I got back to the hotel by late afternoon a uniformed policeman was waiting for me with a large manilla envelope from Inspector Heemskerk. The young man explained that he had been sent to provide a translation of the official notes, and to explain if necessary points of police procedure. On the way up to my room, he admitted that he had been a university graduate and was pleased at the opportunity to practise his English, and I was again impressed with the *élan* that seemed to exist in the Inspector's department.

The investigating team had been thorough, conducting a house-to-house enquiry until they were satisfied they had spoken to everyone who might at some time have overlooked the front or back of van der Meeren's house. Although no one had heard or seen anything unusual on the day of the murder, they had been asked to think back on *any* visitors during the past three months, being pressed for descriptions of even the most nondescript persons.

Taking nothing for granted, making no assumptions of his own, my young companion patiently recited the often vague and frequently conflicting descriptions of some thirteen people — a waste of time as it turned out since eight had been identified subsequently from the volunteered statements of friends and colleagues — leaving only five unaccounted for. Only one of those was in any way distinguishable in a crowd because of his physical appearance — a man, described by a remarkably lucid housewife who had even remembered the light grey suit he wore, as exceptionally tall and thin. I did a hasty sum in my head and estimated that he must have been well over six feet.

The information excited me. Was it more than a coincidence that I had seen a tall, thin man on the day of the auction? Logic warned me that I was clutching at straws. Nevertheless I mentioned the possibility to the policeman, who received the news with sober optimism. "If the man was English he may have stopped at a hotel overnight or longer," I pointed out.

"In which case they would have his passport number," he acknowledged.

"Even if he had arrived the same day by plane or boat-train he may well have used a taxi. Please ask Inspector Heemskerk if he can carry out a check. Someone may have remembered taking a very tall man to the Zwanveld, especially if he spoke to them."

It was a long shot, but the police were obviously thorough, and we had no other leads. And if it was *my* tall man, I intended to do something about it.

THREE

I waited until I had returned to England before contacting Tom Duncan. In the long silence that followed my report and the implied suggestion of a laboratory test, the temperature seemed to drop several degrees; let me just say he was *not* pleased. During the preliminary pleasantries he had made suitably sympathetic noises over the death of van der Meeren, his complacency making it clear he had no idea the Dutch police were unconvinced by the initial robbery theory. By the time I had brought him up to date, the single-mindedness that was so characteric of his buying had taken over. Duncan was a busy man, and not prepared to waste time giving credence to such 'wild' speculation.

"We have a top-notch professor and a third-year research student working on the journal — so obsessed with Emilia Lanier that I practically have to resort to violence to get it back from them at weekends to satisfy our insurance company. You can imagine what they would say about the theory of some smart-assed policeman bucking for promotion."

"For heaven's sake, Tom," I protested. "It took a *murder* to start him thinking in that direction. It's

47

equally possible the manuscript is genuine, and that van der Meeren misappropriated it, or something."

"Or something," he echoed. "In addition to my researchers, you'd do well to remember that the 16th-century happens to be *my* period. When it comes to the other nineteen I might be as thick as two planks, but no one pulls the wool over my eyes when it comes to the 16th, especially the second half." With typical single-mindedness he had conveniently forgotten the 17th century, which I happened to know he regarded with even greater affection.

I suppressed a sigh, bowing to his greater knowledge. "All right, Tom, if that's the way you feel."

"Wait a minute," he interjected angrily. "Since you're paying for this call, I may as well take an extra few minutes to add to your education. You studied the journal; anything strike you about the ink she used?"

"I know very little about inks, but I was rather surprised there was practically no fading. I put that down to the fact that the journal, being very personal, was probably kept in a drawer and remained closed when not in use, which meant it was seldom exposed to light."

"That is correct. But the *intensity* of that black is caused by something called Gum Sandarac, which they used to rub into the paper to stop the ink from 'bleeding' if the sizing didn't cover the paper as well as it might have done — not that unusual in those days. I suspected she had used the stuff when I studied some of the pages under a magnifying glass, so I went prospecting in the crevices where the paper was bound; and sure enough, I came up with a few grains of the stuff buried for 400 years.

48

I bet that surprises you!"

It did, and I admitted it with a feeling of relief. "Then would it not save a lot of possible procrastination later if you carried out the proper tests anyway?"

"Goddam it, man. Either you haven't been listening, or you're a negative sonofabitch who ought to stay out of the saleroom. If you can't believe in yourself or even your associates, you're no use to me — or anyone."

His personal rudeness was unacceptable, and it was with a considerable effort that I managed to control my temper and not slam the phone down; but when I replied the words spilt out stiffly, too icy for fluency. "We'll meet before long, no doubt, and when that happens, the first thing I want — before you say 'Hello' — is an apology. And if I don't think that it's good enough, you'll get my fist down your throat, Golden Gloves or not. I phoned because I feel an obligation to your library, to do what is right, even if it means unpleasantness all round."

There was another pause followed by an embarrassed laugh at the other end. "I don't know what *you're* getting uptight about. Where is that British stiff upper lip we've heard so much about? Besides, this is where the buck stops — at my desk — and since I'm a librarian, not a diplomat, I have to say what I feel. You should know me better than to take it personally."

I snorted, still angry. "Forget it for now — but remember this: the last thing I want is for the Lanier to be a forgery, but if the police theory about the *robbery* being faked is right, then it will look ominous — irrespective of your acknowledged expertise. Experts have been fooled before. No one can force you. The manuscript belongs to you, and you believe what you like — and do what you like. But there may come a time when others raise the question, and your integrity will be open to question."

"It wouldn't come to that," he responded gruffly.

"*I* know that, but the ball is in your court."

"Look, Matt," he protested, his voice rising again with anger. "Nobody is going to tell me that my baby is a fake. You've only glanced at it — I've read every word, and I will have to be confronted with the forger in person, and then interrogate him under the lie-detector before I even start to take you seriously. If you or anyone thinks that Tom Duncan is going to allow some vandal in the guise of a lab technician to take even a one-thousandth of an inch of that precious paper, you're crazy."

I knew how he felt, so there was little point in commenting. I sighed and for a moment wished I had never heard of Emilia Lanier. "At least I told you," I concluded tamely.

There was another awkward silence before he tried to repair our damaged relationship with a chuckle, but it was strained. "You sure did. Don't worry, and remember: faint heart never won Dark Lady."

He was probably right.

I tried to put the whole soured episode out of my mind, but my conscience would not allow me to reject van der Meeren. In Heemskerk's office I had seen a photograph, and I had built up a mental picture of a dull, rather anonymous sort of man who may have strayed from the academic path in response to a sudden temptation. According to Heemskerk, there were indications that the professor had been

50

restless during the past year or so, although perhaps no more than the soul searching that afflicts so many people in middle age — what had he achieved in life? what more could he expect in the years he had left? Money seemed an unlikely incentive; attention was perhaps something else. We would probably never know. Perhaps as Van der Bogaarde had suggested, the manuscript had belonged to someone else, and the professor a convenient figurehead; not even a thief, but an accessory after the fact.

After ten days I had to accept the fact that the Dutch police had failed to add substance to the theory that 'my' tall man was English. Either I could wait in the hope that Heemskerk's obvious thoroughness eventually unearthed fresh evidence, or simply give up. That was hard to accept, but I had nowhere to start — apart from proceeding on the assumption that the manuscript had been forged in this country, and trying to reconstruct how it might have been carried out. The idea began to appeal to me, especially as I was able to convince myself that with a little self-discipline they were the sort of enquiries that should not take up too much of my time.

I concentrated on the physical obstacles to producing a book that could pass for being 400 years old, with all the differences in manufacturing techniques. The binding was, relatively, the easiest consideration since the materials used were still basically the same, and the various dyes would not present an insurmountable obstacle; writing ink again could be manufactured to early specification on record, and although I would need to speak to a calligrapher about styles and pens, these were problems that could easily be overcome by the dedicated forger, who presumably already knew something about the art.

Getting the paper right was a much greater headache. Whatever skills and techniques employed, he would have to start by finding a source of handmade paper — either, if he was incredibly lucky, the endpapers of genuine books or notebooks of the period, or by matching paper made today by the traditional method, and then appropriately 'aged'. I discounted the first, failing to see how even an antiquarian bookseller could rustle up a sufficient quantity of the same size for the purpose; still less a thief tearing out endpapers from books at the British or other antiquarian libraries. Ticket-holders may not be kept under constant observation, but it would be risky trying to remove *one* endpaper in an open reading-room, let alone hundreds.

I concentrated instead on the second possibility, more difficult to fake, but perfectly feasible with the right degree of knowledge and dedication. I was not an expert, but from my experience in the book trade I had a general picture of the history of paper, and was able to supplement this information from the various reference books I kept at hand.

From pre-printing days to 1799, when the first machine for producing a continuous web of paper was introduced, paper was made by hand in basically the same way — from rags soaked in water and bleach and crushed into a fibrous state in a pulp vat. The mixture was more than 90% water, and the paper-maker's skill lay mainly in getting just the correct consistency for the quality and weight of paper required. A wooden framed mould with thin wires strung across in a close-runged effect, would be dipped into an open vat containing the thin porridge mixture. When the pulp had been very skilfully spread evenly across the mould, the outer frame was removed and the fresh 'paper' turned out like a pancake, being placed between layers of felt and blanket so that most of the water could be removed in a screw press. The paper would then be hung up to dry thoroughly over a period, after which it would be coated with an animal-based size to provide a smooth surface and to prevent the ink from 'bleeding' or penetrating too far; finally it would be glazed by rolling between sheets of polished zinc. Paper needed for handwriting, such as in this case, would have a harder surface than that used for print. A further demarcation line came in 1840 when wood pulp was introduced. Watermarks (made from small metal moulds attached to the wire of the paper-mould) also had to be contended with, but these were not difficult to copy or fake if one had access to historical records.

Frensham gave me the name of a paper expert in London, and I brought forward my next visit to call in at her fascinating little shop in Covent Garden. With her help I identified the type and weight of paper most likely to have been used by a forger, although she was sceptical that it could be aged well enough to fool the experts. However, when I told her that Frensham and other distinguished experts had admitted they would have been tricked if my theory was correct, she conceded that possibility if they had come to the evaluation 'cold' and not on their guard. Finally, she gave me the names of three mills where hand-made paper is still produced; her advice that England was one of the few countries in Europe still maintaining the traditional craft (and she specifically dismissed Holland) narrowing the field considerably. One, the largest of the mills, was quickly ruled out when I began making enquiries, because they accepted special orders only in very large quantities; they would not have sold less than for a run of several hundred books.

I then wrote formally to the other suppliers, John Bromsgrove & Sons, of Sevenoaks, Kent, and Hodgkinson's paper-mill at Wookey Hole, the famous caves in Somerset, giving them the paper's specification and asking if they could let me have the names of any customers for that type of paper in the past three years. I followed up with a telephone call, giving Frensham's name as a reference, and ended up with a list of seven names, all printers.

Ideally I should have visited all seven, because the information I got from them over the phone was inevitably skimpy, and there was little to indicate whether or not they were really telling the truth. But three of them were in the far north of England, and I was reluctant to spend any more time on this line of enquiry until I had a general impression from the initial telephone communication. In each case they were able to recall the order, and link it to a specific print project − mostly private press or expensive limited editions. On the fifth call, to Bernard Tarrant & Son of St Albans, Hertforshire, I had been referred to the managing director, John Tarrant, who was away, but he returned my call the next day.

"I understand you have been trying to reach me. How can I help?" he enquired.

I thanked him for taking the trouble to call back, and explained that I had been given his name by the Wookey Hole mill. "I'm trying to find someone who bought a certain quality of paper from them − the sort that might be used for . . . " There are a number of occasions, apart from private press work, when a printer might wish to use hand-made paper that was 'in character', so while I could not be completely frank, there was no need for an elaborate cover-story. ". . . matching a piece of old print, say 17th and 18th century . . . ?"

Tarrant was as spontaneously helpful as the others had been. "Yes, that would be me. Why, are you in the market for a few sheets?"

"My problem is that I don't want many — just looking for a few left-overs. Do you think you might be able to help?"

"I should think so; no use to me now the job's finished. Why do you want them? Are you a printer?"

I hesitated, wishing I knew a little more about the man at the other end, and visualising an earnest little printer trying to be helpful. I was not in a position to tell the truth, irrespective of who and what he was, yet I was beginning to feel self-conscious about the implausibility of my story. A genuine printer requiring only a few sheets would hardly do all this detective work when he could buy from a specialist paper merchant for the cost of a single phone call. Yet while there was the possibility that the man at the other end had something to hide, I had to be vague. I decided to change my tack. "Your voice is rather familiar, Mr Tarrant — *and* the name. I'm sure we've met before. I'm a bookseller. Does it ring a bell at all?"

"Can't say it does, Mr Coll. I don't meet many booksellers — *publishers*. If you had said 'publishers' it might have done."

"It's just a feeling. You wouldn't have a pretty heavy beard — " I laughed with mock self-consciousness — "well built? What might be described as a 'fine figure of a man'?"

His laugh seemed more natural than mine. "Hardly. Not even a moustache. And no one could call me 'well built'. On the contrary I'm very tall and thinner than my doctor would like."

My heart leapt. *Coll, you're a genius,* I told myself, and my brain raced to press home the advantage. "I've got a few very old books that need a little restoration work, just the odd page here and there. If I go to the top specialists it will cost me a fortune, and I've got a brilliant young student who can do the work, but doesn't have access to some of the materials, such as this sort of paper. According to Mr Johnson your order seems just right, and I only want a few sheets."

"By all means," Tarrant replied helpfully. "I can probably spare a dozen or so if you are sure they're really what you want. I can put them in the post with an invoice – price I paid, plus a nominal handling charge."

While I wanted a sample sheet for possible comparison later, I also had a great desire to meet the man face to face. "That would be wonderful," I hedged. "But perhaps I had better take a look before committing myself. Could I call in over the next few days?"

There was a pause while he appeared to consult his diary. "I shan't be here myself, Mr Coll, but I can leave the package with an assistant."

I cursed under my breath. "Oh – no panic, I suppose. I'd like to say 'hello' at the same time. I can leave it until you are back in the office."

"Where are you speaking from."

"Ardley, in Dorset."

He reflected. "No point in you coming all the way over here, Mr Coll. Bad enough if we were in London, but my premises are well over an hour's drive on top of that. Look, I.ve got to go down to the West Country day after tomorrow after some potential business, and while I'm there I intended to pop in to Wookey Hole to discuss a special order. It wouldn't take you more than a couple of hours to nip across country. Why don't we meet at the paper-mill at, say, 5 o'clock? They close about that time, but I'm well known down there so you can have a quick look before we leave — it's something of a tourist attraction, you know — and then we can have a beer somewhere."

I agreed, trying to conceal my delight at how convenient it was turning out. Of course, there was just the possibility Tarrant might turn out to be just another tall, thin man — but I had a strong hunch I was on the right track. I recalled the way he had stared at me, and the girl — what was her name? Yes, Charlotte Hesse — the way he had stared at one or other of us in the 'Mason's Arms', and in the street afterwards. I savoured the prospect of watching his reaction when I confronted him; Mr Tarrant would have a rude shock in the next 24 hours.

The drive to Wookey Hole, via the lovely city of Wells, was pleasant. One of the advantages of living in the country is the different perspective it gives to driving which becomes an occasion to relax, in drama-tic contrast to the pressure-pot atmosphere of Lon-don's traffic. The only jam one encountered in my neck of the woods was the infrequent monopolisa-tion of a single-lane road by a local farmer's tractor. But even then with air that was razor sharp in its freshness, and — corny though it sounds — the birds twittering in the trees; any trees, but all with bark that was grey and not filthy black in common, blood pressure stuck at a healthy norm. Initially I had been preoccupied with the slow-dying habits of London, and tended to be only vaguely aware of the scenery and its constituent parts, but it had not taken me more than a month or so to unwind.

It was getting dark when I arrived. Out of the tourist season, there did not seem to be many people about, and there were fewer than a dozen vehicles in the huge car park where I left the Citroen. I discovered that the guided tour of the paper-mill also took in the caves, and other intriguing novelties such as Madame Tussaud's store-room, and wondered whether I might 'charm' someone into admitting me free in view of the time of day. It transpired that the office was already closed, although I could see lights in the restaurant, so there were obviously some staff as well as visitors still around. I made a token effort to find someone in authority, and then, anxious not to keep Tarrant waiting, made my way to the signposted paper-mill. Approached by a bridge straddling a small valley, the entrance on an upper floor was through the old part of the mill, now apparently a museum, and down into the main production area, fully lit but totally deserted.

I looked at my watch; it was past 5 o'clock, and I realised the staff had probably finished for the day, which was not in itself surprising, except that I could have expected to see the manager or head paper-maker around — if only because Tarrant's visit which was, after all, supposed to be on a business matter. There was no sign of him either, which was especially irritating. I was torn between anger at his apparent unreliability and the wasted journey it had caused, and disappointment at missing the opportunity to see a traditional manufacturing process.

I was obliged to wait anyway at least until someone switched off the lights (it was possible that Tarrant had been delayed *en route*, although at this time of year traffic was not heavy), so I wandered back to the main work-room, in which the current paper-making activities take place. The working area was set out on what seemed like a sunken floor with a railed platform surrounding it on three sides — presumably for the benefit of visitors. It was dominated by a metal pulp vat, approximately 6 ft long and 4 ft wide, at one end, and a screw press at the other, with the freshly produced sheets of paper being laid out between. The vat was almost full of a white substance which could have been mistaken for paint — or on closer inspection, semolina, and was presumably all that remained of the processed cotton, used today instead of rags.

As my eyes followed what I took to be the sequence of manufacture, I noticed for the first time that there was a man sitting in a chair, obscured by the vat and the filler apparatus above. Wearing brown overalls over his working-clothes and a brown protective hat, he appeared to be entering various calculations on a clipboard resting on his lap. I realised he was a member of the staff who, intent on his figure-work, had not heard me come in. For all I knew, he might have been warned to expect me, and even at this moment he wondering why I was delayed, so I introduced myself: "Excuse me. I'm waiting to meet a Mr Tarrant here."

Obviously I had not been expected and it was impossible to say whether Tarrant's name meant anything to him either, because he merely nodded indifferently before returning to his calculations.

"I'm sorry to disturb you," I interjected again, "but may I come down for a closer look while I'm waiting?"

Since he was far too wrapped up in his figures to bother with me, I climbed through the rail and dropped a couple of feet to the work-level. I was interested in the whole process, but particularly the moulds and the consistency of the mixture, and for the moment was so preoccupied that Tarrant was forgotten. The workman did not move from his chair until I was actually standing by the vat, and the sight of me surreptitiously dipping a finger in, and generally behaving like a member of the public who was bound to do something stupid, must have reminded him of a rule about allowing strangers to wander about unchaperoned. Reluctantly he got up to protect his interests. I did not so much see him approach as to become aware of his presence. Sitting down, hunched up had been deceptive; standing now only a couple of steps away he seemed freakishly tall, although on reflection probably no more than three or four inches taller than my six feet. I was probably also disorientated by the anonymity of the brown overalls, but he did not seem quite as emaciated as I had remembered, yet there was no doubt this was my staring man. In that split second I realised I had walked into a trap; I should have realised on the telephone the moment he decided to volunteer what he looked like — as though a printer with any business sense at all would have put himself out to arrange a meeting which might just result in the sale of a few sheets of blank paper! The idea was so ludicrous I cursed myself for being so complacent to imagine that *I* had led *him* into a trap.

Tarrant looked down at me with a half smile that was faintly menacing, although I could not justify the feeling. Then I remembered. While there was nothing actually wrong with his teeth, the expression reminded me for a moment of 'Jaws', one of James Bond's adversaries — the giant with the teeth of steel. There is no reason for me to be scared of anyone physically — but I was momentarily disconcerted, and I was still trying to think of a suitably cool remark, when he kicked me across the shins.

Years before I had been trained not to react to pain, but I was so unprepared, and the pain so intense that it drowned my other senses. I did what anyone would have done — lifted my injured right leg off the ground and clutched at it protectively. That momentary loss of concentration was enough to put me at a disadvantage. He dived for the other leg, lifted and pushed me back against the vat. Nothing is more disorientating than loss of balance, and the metal edge scraping into my lower back was almost reassuringly real — until I was off the ground and leaving it behind. I had the presence of mind to clutch at the hat he was wearing, but he shook it off, let go of my left leg and used both hands to push down on my shoulders. Suddenly I knew I was about to dive backwards into the white pool. I took a breath, closed my eyes, and went under.

It was the colour and relative thickness of the mixture which saved my life. If it had been water, he would not have lost sight of me, and managed to prevent me from coming up for air. As it was I emerged at an angle that caught him napping, and blindly grabbed hold of the side of the vat. Tarrant lashed out at my knuckles with the heel of his shoe and I was forced to let go, but now I could at least

61

stand up in the pulp, waist deep. We stared at each other like two wild animals pawing at the ground with rage, but he realised that without the element of surprise it would be almost impossible to drown me without a prolonged struggle, and sooner or later someone would come to investigate. He hesitated, looking for a weapon that would make all the difference, but then the decision was made for him — we heard a door bang in the distance and someone approaching.

Tarrant waited no longer, darting through the only side that had no railings, into an intercommunicating room and then out — judging by the echoing sound — through one of the many emergency exits. I could hear footsteps, the sound of men running towards me, and climbed wearily out of the vat. The pain in my shins was now just a dull ache, but my knuckles felt as thugh they were broken.

The US Cavalry, or whoever they were, seemed to take ages to arrive, and I doubted if there was much chance of them finding Tarrant outside in the dark, especially as he was too sensible to simply drive off. Then the echoing footsteps suddenly stopped, and three men entered the room; two uniformed policemen, just ahead of a white-haired man in a blue pinstripe suit; I assumed he was something to do with the mill. The peaked caps of the younger men identified them as a squad-car unit which meant that someone had dialled 999, but they were not as imperturbable as one comes to expect — stopping dead in front of the railings above me, as though scared of coming too close, trying not to laugh at the sight of the white apparition. My solemn expression, accentuated by the weight of gunge on eyebrows and cheeks — it may have looked like semolina but it felt like cement — must have made me look like an extra in a Laurel and Hardy film, and for a split second even I saw the funny side of it. However, an increasing awareness of the throbbing pain in my left hand pushed any vestige of humour aside, and my spirits hit rock bottom. The fact that my clothes were obviously ruined added to the alarming sense of helplessness, and taking advantage of my sagging morale the dozens of petty worries, in themselves totally unimportant, threatened to overwhelm me — where could I get clean, a change of clothes; ·vas I covered by insurance, how would I explain?

I don't know whether the policemen expected me to shake myself like a dog, but they maintained a respectful distance; heaven knows what would have happened if I had needed assistance, let alone the kiss of life. The nearer one suddenly came out of his trance enquiring: "What happened to you?" He was a plump young man, with a baby face accentuated by an incongruous moustache that was obviously a mistaken attempt to give credence to his adult-hood. In fact, he looked as ludicrous as a Keystone cop, which made him an ideal foil for me, although his companion, probably about the same age, seemed to have a little more authority. He, at least, had taken the trouble to inspect the outer rooms.

"You won't believe this," I said, "but someone *pushed* me in."

The third man, who might have been the manager judging by his age and concerned expression, as though idiot tourists were frequently falling in the vats, interrupted reassuringly: "I found one of our employees tied up, and called the police. Presumably, whoever did that must have attacked you."

I nodded. "Can I get out of these clothes somewhere?"

"My name is Bereton," he said, "I should have some clothes to fit you. I don't live very far away."

The plump young constable looked worried, as though he was about to witness the destruction of vital evidence. "Better report in first, sir. Headquarters will put out an alert for the man who attacked you."

"You do that," I replied, "while I go and change."

We were joined by his companion who seemed to take charge. "We shall need a description, sir. But first we have to make sure you're not hurt. It seems like a pretty savage attack. Did you get hit on the head at all?" He came to within a few inches of me and looked into my eyes, although I turned away irritably. "Sorry, sir, but the villain can wait a couple of extra minutes — he won't get far if we set up road-blocks. But you could be suffering from concussion, almost certainly delayed shock."

He noticed the way I favoured my left hand, took the wrist gently and examined the knuckles. He pulled a face. "Something probably broken there — needs an X-ray."

I conceded in the face of his concern. "Do what you like — as long as I can get out of these clothes."

He nodded. "We've got a blanket in the car. That'll keep you reasonably warm on the way to the hospital." He turned on his heel sharply as though conscious of the fact that enough time had been wasted. I felt obliged to wipe clean the mental graffiti about young policemen; even the fat buffoon suddenly seemed more businesslike — perhaps it was just appearance that was against him.

I thanked Bereton for his kind offer of clothes, but suggested I could probably get something at the hospital, and the sooner we got there the better. I followed the policemen out and slumped into the back of the police Rover, while one of them reported on the car radio. I looked dispiritedly out of the window and saw my Citroen, another 'loose end' to be sorted out later.

Actually sitting down at last in the car, the aches and pains asserted themselves. I was conscious again of the bruises on my shins, and the pain around my knuckles became intense. To complete my misery, I started to shiver, although I did not know whether this was because I was still in wet clothes, or delayed shock. I leaned back in the seat, eyes closed, conscious of the sludge on my uncovered head marking the seat, but too tired to care.

The fat one was driving, and his companion turned to face me, his right arm resting on the back of his seat. "You must be feeling terrible, sir, but we need a description of the man who attacked you."

Despite the physical discomfort by making the effort I was still able to think clearly. I could not only give a description, but a name and address. My pride put a brake on that train of thought. I could not give Tarrant the satisfaction of knowing he had outwitted me — quite apart from the fact that I might have been killed. I knew where I could reach him, and was determined that nothing should prevent me catching up with him. There was, of course, the risk that he might panic and not return home, but I suspected that a man of his cunning would have a cover-story prepared, and remain confident in his ability to talk his way out of any apparently wild accusations. It was down to me. All I needed was time, because when the local police began to investigate the matter they would soon learn of my initial

65

enquiry about special paper orders, and the customers involved, and would want to know what had motivated my visit that afternoon.

However, for the time being, I could use my dazed condition as an excuse. "It all happened so suddenly, I can't remember," I said convincingly. "I think he was tall — quite a bit taller than me, but that's all. It was over in a flash.

I reckoned I was obliged to mention Tarrant's height in case the employee who had been attacked proved to have a better memory. Luckily the young policeman was inexperienced enough to allow his sympathy to sway his judgement, and did not pursue the matter, more especially what I was doing at the mill at that time of day. I then dictated a formal, very vague, statement which I promised to read through and sign as soon as I was able.

A hot shower at the hospital made me feel immeasurably better. The paper-pulp, despite the bleach content, had not damaged my skin in any way, although there were a few white streaks in my hair where it had dried and refused to melt again for merely cosmetic reasons. While someone was rustling up some clothes, I was taken to X-ray, and the break confirmed. I should have been resigned to the worst, but was not prepared for the consequences — which meant that within seconds of having one plaster-like mixture washed off, I was given a new, much thicker dressing, enclosing practically the whole of my left hand. I protested that I would not be able to use my car, and would be stranded 'hundreds' of miles from home, but immediately began to feel ungracious at making a fuss after all the trouble I had given them. I swallowed my concern and accepted a bed for the night.

After nearly nine hours' sleep I was again fit for action, and could not wait to get at Tarrant — despite the fact I had no car. I telephoned Mr Bereton to ask if I could still, freshly scrubbed, take advantage of his offer of clothes that were rather more suitable than the slacks and sweater provided by the hospital, so that I could go into Wells or somewhere and hire an automatic car, which would overcome the problem of a left hand that was practically rigid. Then I phoned Charlie Appleton and asked him to help out at the shop at short notice; I had a young assistant most days, but for any length of time I worried about it being left without proper supervision — and Charlie knew more about the business than anyone.

"I have to go to London urgently," I told him, "but if anyone you don't know rings for me, say that I'm confined to bed, and that the doctor says I am not to be disturbed." I hoped that Tarrant would try to check up, and that such a message might sound convincing.

"What are you up to?" demanded Charlie.

"Now don't nag, Charlie. I shall be all right." I was on the point of asking him to arrange to get my Citroen back to Ardley, but that would have involved an even more complicated explanation, and since he tended to behave like my father I did not wish to worry him. Besides, I could collect it when I returned the automatic. If the cast was not pliable enough in a couple of days I would break the damn thing!

FOUR

Since the start of my love affair with Ardley, and Dorset in general, I had become selective in where I travelled, given the choice. I've nothing against towns like Walsall and Warrington, but in the same way as I admire character and class in books, and women, I prefer to limit my social and book-buying trips to places that would in themselves give me some form of aesthetic satisfaction. St Albans is that sort of city, and mentally I congratulated Tarrant on his good fortune, although I had no idea why he lived and worked there; in all probability he had merely taken over his father's business. But whatever his shortcomings, Tarrant was obviously not lacking in ambition; indeed, a man possibly involved in a large-scale fraud, and who reacted so very 'positively' to potential danger, was not someone to be underestimated. And my first impression of his printing-works, just off the main Watford Road, but set back in a secluded spot almost within sight of the Roman wall to the north, confirmed that view: a 2,000-square foot modern ground-floor building, built on to a large and attractive three-storey Victorian house, was not especially impressive, but for the type of work I knew he did represented a healthy-looking operation.

In reception, a middle-aged woman secretary, told me that Tarrant was 'out of town' on business, but that his assistant, Jim Walsh, could probably deal with my enquiry. I wondered where Tarrant was — still in the West Country, maintaining his 'alibi' schedule? Or gone to ground? The former was the likelier bet; he was not the sort of man to overreact, even to the very real possibility that I had identified him to the police, and in some ways it was convenient that I could take a dispassionate look at his home without him on hand to raise my blood pressure.

Mr Walsh, a respectful but warm man in his late fifties, was typical of so many printing-house foremen, extremely knowledgeable, but without the veneer of sophistication that rubs off on many successful printers in the constant struggle to get business. I informed him that I was a publisher looking for an efficient printing operation to handle two of my smaller circulation quality magazines, and accepted his eager invitation to look over the works. It seemed their work was predominantly letterpress, and they had seven machines and a dozen employees. But while he extolled the virtues of their undoubtedly efficient operation, I was looking for means of access to the house. I did not relish the prospect with my injured hand of climbing up a drain-pipe and through an upstairs window, when it was probable Tarrant normally used an internal door. The one-level modern building would not present the same problem, since there was nothing movable inside, and therefore an unlikely target for thieves, to present a security risk.

I did not have to look far to spot two doors,

apparently unlocked, that Tarrant might use for convenience. Even if they were locked at night, they would not present a serious obstacle. But I was on the point of leaving when I realised I had made a sweeping assumption that Tarrant lived alone, and that I would have the house to myself. Luckily my good fortune held. To my innocent question: Was there a *Mrs* Tarrant? Walsh needed no urging to relate much of the Tarrant family history; that there *had* been a Mrs Tarrant who had left home some years before. His employer was now the only occupant of the house since the death of his parents, but it did not seem empty since Tarrant's library alone occupied two large rooms, and another was designated a games-room, complete with full-size snooker-table. He made it all sound like the blurb on the brochure for a stately home, and was obviously impressed with his employer's life-style. All that interested me was that I need have no fear of disturbing the occupants, although it did occur to me in passing that anyone with that number of books could not be *all* that bad.

I should explain in case I've inadvertently projected a note of complacency, that I had been trained in forcible entry during my Service days in intelligence, and it was not a question of how to get in, but how quickly it would take. I killed time in the afternoon by visiting the Roman remains at Verulamium, and then going to the cinema where I spent the first half-hour wondering whether I had been overcharged, before realising that my shock at the price was merely a reflection of the number of years since I had last been. At 10.30 p.m. I drove back to within a few hundred yards of the Tarrant works, and then walked

70

the rest of the way. The place was in darkness, and there was not a light to be seen from the buildings near by, which happily reduced the risk of being seen. I had carried out my preliminary reconnaissance earlier, and went like bee to honey straight to the back of the building where I was reasonably sure that a narrow metal framed window at head height belonged to the mens' lavatory. I was mildly surprised that anyone had bothered to close it, but had come prepared. During the afternoon I had purchased a roll of wide black insulating tape from a hardware store, and now I spread it generously across the pane of glass. I used the heel of my shoe to break the glass, and then lifted out the loose sections, enough to insert my hand and release the lever-handle. The opening was not large, but more than enough, even with my handicap.

Safely inside the building, I knew I was separated from the large machine-shop at the front by a smaller storeroom and office area. I doubted whether Tarrant would keep anything of any relevance to my search down here, but it would be foolish not to carry out at least a token search. I had a powerful hand-torch which had come with the car, and did not intend to turn on the lights unless I found something worthy of special interest in a desk-drawer or filing-cabinet. The offices were unlocked for the benefit of the cleaners, judging from the empty metal waste-bins left on top of the desks, and a name-plate identified Tarrant's private office, treated no differently from the rest.

Going through the drawers quickly but systematically, it never entered my head that everything had gone with suspiciously smooth routine, and when the main overhead lights went on I was stunned. Momentarily my eyes had difficulty in adjusting to the brightness, but the size of the silhouette outlined a few feet away made it obvious that the newcomer was Tarrant. My eyes were 'assisted' too by the shotgun he held, which quickly came into focus crystal clear. When I looked up he was smiling expansively, which made him almost personable.

"Dear me, a burglar," he remarked with mock surprise. "The grey woolly gloves don't look very professional, if you don't mind me being personal."

Despite my embarrassment at being caught out again, I found myself smiling at his sense of humour. "I didn't think anyone would notice in the dark." I raised my left hand and removed the glove to reveal the plaster-cast. "Not easy finding something to fit . . ." His eyes glinted at the injury, and I wanted desperately to hurt him, but I was able to conceal the anger and settled for a mild: "What kept you?"

He looked hurt. "Be fair. I was in the West Country until mid-afternoon. Decided to leave when Mrs Gibbons told me about the too-good-to-be-true new business prospect. I thought the least I could do was to be on hand to play the hospitable host."

"I thought we ought to get better acquainted after that unfortunate incident at Wookey Hole. I can't believe you really meant me to drown in the vat?"

He grinned. "I don't stand on ceremony I'm afraid. But I don't know what you must have thought of me; I'm not usually such a bungler. Fortunately, on my home ground I'm a tougher proposition."

I looked at the gun. "Must you point that in my direction?" I held up my left hand pathetically. "I didn't come looking for trouble, and now that I'm here I can't see why we shouldn't converse in a civilised manner."

Tarrant shook his head. "The stakes are too high, if you'll pardon the cliché. You know too much." He shrugged and laughed. "Oh dear, that sounds even worse."

I shrugged. "I don't *know* anything. I might suspect you, but I can't prove anything. Whatever you've been up to, I'm not interested in anything except the Lanier journal, and I've got a horrible sinking feeling that you've master-minded, organised, led, inspired, carried out, or whatever, a pretty clever fraud."

The surprise in his face looking genuine enough. "I don't know what you're talking about — I've never set eyes on the journal."

"So it was just coincidence you happened to be at the auction?"

"It was. And if you're now telling me you bought a forgery, it's news to me. Hard luck!"

"You deserve an Oscar, Tarrant. I take my hat off to you."

"Shut up," he ordered. "Do you think I'm so thick that I'm going to break down and confess everything because you fancy yourself as Perry Mason? I don't know anything about the journal, but as I said at the beginning, *you're* obviously a burglar. When I call the police I shall have to admit I fired, but that I didn't aim to *kill*. It was dark; I was scared, and when I called out to you I took it for granted you would stop. Even then I fired at your legs. I guess I'm just not used to firing the damn thing."

I could see he was deadly serious, but such cold-blooded ruthlessness was still hard to accept. "It's not as easy as that, Tarrant," I warned. "In the normal way you would be lucky to escape a manslaughter charge, but with me that charge must be murder."

He sneered. "Don't tell me you're not alone — the place is really surrounded by police?"

"No, but equally I'm not that stupid to break in here without protecting my rear. I paid the penalty of underestimating you — twice. Don't you fall into the same trap and underestimate me."

"A trap, is it?" he enquired cockily, but his expression belied his confidence.

"I've spoken to *two* detectives about you," I began with a half-truth. "Inspector Heemskerk in Holland, because of one of van der Meeren's neighbours reported seeing a very tall, thin man, and I remembered you from the auction."

"Pull the other one," he sneered, but I could see my desperate talk was beginning to unnerve him.

"The other was a personal friend at Ardley CID. I gave him an off-the-record account of what happened at Wookey Hole, because I wouldn't have known where to start with the local police. How d'you think he would react if I was found shot only a few hours later?"

"Police deal in facts. I'm prepared to take my chance," he retorted edgily. "Get out of that chair and over to the door."

I shrugged helplessly, walked round the side of the desk, and with my right hand swung the metal bin on top towards the gun-barrel. The gun went off, but the charge was deflected into the wall and I closed with him. Conscious of my injured hand, he did not bother to defend himself, concentrating instead on lining up the gun again. My only hope was to do the unexpected. I used my plaster-encased hand, fingers stiff as a spear, and jabbed at his eyes from his 'blind'

74

side. Tarrant cried out with pain and shock, and staggered back. I stood off clinically and measured him for a kick to the testicles. This time the pain was so deep rooted that the scream seemed to freeze in his throat. When he slumped to the ground I knew I would have no more trouble from him for several hours.

I unloaded the gun's other chamber and completed my search of the desk while he lay on the floor and stared at me through inflamed eyes that watered like a leaking faucet, face expressionless apart from the occasional partially controlled spasm of pain. He would not give me the satisfaction of even an involuntary groan, and despite my indifference to his suffering I had to admire his stoicism. As I had anticipated there was nothing of interest in the office, and I decided to concentrate on the house. I retrieved the gun and pointed it at him. "Get up!"

He ignored me, so I rammed the barrel into his midriff as a painful reminder that a shotgun does not need ammunition to be a dangerous weapon. He was still suffering the effects of the kick, and it took him more than five minutes to roll over on to his knees and pull himself up by the door-handle. The waves of pain and nausea reflected in his face, despite the tightly shut eyes, were so graphic I could almost sense what appeared to be waves of black energy. I let him take his time, since it was preferable to carrying him, and made him lead the way into his house, switching off the lights behind us.

"You're wasting your time," he said, speaking with an effort. "You won't find anything." I ignored him until we had reached the foot of a grand circular staircase, where he stopped. "It's a big house," he said.

"We'll start with your study."

Tarrant shook his head, despite the morale-sapping pain beginning to regain his assurance. "I work in the office."

"Then we'll try *every* room."

He groaned. "Give me credit for some intelligence, Coll. Do I look the sort of person to leave incriminating evidence around?"

He did not, but I could not afford to trust him. Ordering him to turn round, his back to me and wrists outstretched I secured them with the insulating tape. I used most of the roll until I was confident I could get on with the search without constantly looking over my shoulder. Even a karate expert cannot kick effectively without using his hands for counter-balance.

My search was clinically thorough, with the two bathrooms, kitchen and games-room coming in for as much attention as the living-rooms. After an hour wih nothing to show for it, logic began to erode my self-confidence. After all, I reasoned, if Tarrant was involved in dishonest dealings, I would not know what constituted evidence, if I was lucky enough to find it. Bank statements, with large sums paid in, or out? I was not in a position to challenge even the strangest explanations. On the other hand, I was only concerned with the Lanier journal, and what evidence was a forged manuscript likely to leave in its wake? There was no printer's type involved, and it would be a miracle if I came across any papers and inks that might have been used.

I might have given up had it not been for Tarrant. One would have expected his spirits to rise in direct relation to the drop in mine, yet his edginess increased with each 'clean' room, until by the time we got to his bedroom his manner was practically a give-away. The drawer to his bedside cabinet was locked — the first encouraging sign, and when I had forced it I found a small pile of letters, and a photograph. I was conscious of uttering a sigh of relief and looking up at him with a smile — and feeling even better as he turned away in disgust. The letters were a red (on reflection, *blue*) herring; they were of an intimate nature from three or four different women, and I glanced through them hurriedly, tempted to dwell on certain passages of a more lascivious nature, but not allowing myself to be distracted. There was nothing in them relevant to my search, and I put them back; while, in the cupboard section below there was a pile of 'girlie' magazines of a fairly bland type — altogether nothing really surprising for a batchelor's bedroom. The photograph was something else — a Polaroid colour still of Charlotte Hesse, fractionally out of focus, in head and shoulders. She was looking straight at the camera with a half-smile, and although she looked darker than in real life, the effect was attractive, even erotic. I held it up for his benefit.

He shrugged. "You won't believe me, whatever I say. It's an illustration for a brochure we're printing. You can see she's wearing a knitted woollen cardigan made from my customer's wool." He tailed off tamely.

I shook my head. "You were right. Try again."

He looked sheepish. "It's personal. I like women. They're my hobby, as you'll have noticed. I collect photographs when I can get them."

"I'm not interested in women in general, just this one. How well d'you know her?"

He shook his head. "I don't. It's just another fantasy."

I sneered. "Don't tell me it's one of those trick

77

pictures. Put on special glasses and the clothes disappear?"

He flushed with irritation, or perhaps it was humiliation. "Everything in this room is personal — nothing to do with any wheeling and dealing I might, or might not, get up to."

"You know *who* she is?"

He nodded.

"But just 'admire her from afar', as they say?"

He nodded again. "I did try to introduce myself once, but she didn't want to know."

It was the first statement he had made that had a note of truth about it. "So you spy on her from time to time," I said, "when you can find the time?" He did not reply, his silence a tacit admission, so I turned the screw. "*When* d'you find the time? A busy man like you has to plan his diary engagements. Was it just a coincidence you turned up at the auction on the day we first set eyes on each other?"

"I'm interested in books, as you can see from the library, so when it's convenient I go to the occasional sale. I choose the major ones because there's a chance she will be there for her newspaper. I was lucky on that occasion."

His story seemed plausible, too plausible. "I'll tell you what I think," I announced, putting the photograph back in the drawer. "You're in it together. I don't know which is the chicken and which is the egg, but you proved the technical know-how; she wrote the diary. She seemed to know a helluva lot about Emilia Lander."

"What about untying my hands?" he complained. "I'm getting cramp."

"I concede I haven't got a scrap of evidence," I said, ignoring the appeal, "but surely you've con-

78

victed yourself a dozen times over. I paid you the compliment before of assuming you wouldn't over-react to the danger I might talk to the police. Yet, on reflection, that is precisely what you did from the beginning — overreacted."

"You're quite right. I'd done nothing wrong, but when you started making enquiries I must have panicked. When in doubt, do nothing should be the rule — but I'm a restless person; I have to do *something*."

"But *murder* can't be dismissed as simply 'something'. Unless you happen to be a homicidal maniac, I doubt whether even you would have tried to kill me *twice*, unless you had a pretty big investment to protect."

"I was only trying to frighten you: I would have been mad to have shot you on my own doorstep and had the police crawling about the place."

I smiled. "All right: tried to kill me *once*. And if it wasn't my journal, and we're really talking at cross-purposes, it would have to be something equally valuable. Don't tell me you've been forging bank-notes?"

"Look, Mr Coll," he said in a more reasonable tone. "I'm not admitting anything as a matter of principle, and naturally you'll never prove anything, but let's just say that I'm not very happy with you breathing down my neck at all times of the day and night. There's an old saying — if you can't beat 'em, join 'em. Now, there's nothing to actually join, so the least you can do is — let sleeping dogs lie. No one is going to thank you for trying to prove you've sold them a pup. So, forget about that un-fortunate misunderstanding at Wookey Hole, and get back to your shop."

"And?"

"And there'll be a little something for your trouble."

"Such as?"

He appeared to give it some thought. "I did ruin your suit, of course. And you had all that unnecessary expense in Holland. Let's say £2,000?"

The line of enquiry seemed to have come to a dead-end. "I'll think it over," I replied, and started to leave.

"What about my hands?"

I walked past him, and down the stairs. At the bottom I turned and looked up at him. "Sorry, but I shouldn't have hit you with my bad hand — it's throbbing like mad. I'll have to rest it."

FIVE

On leaving St Albans, I toyed with the idea of a slight detour through London to spend the night at Laura Cottingham's flat, a stone's throw from Marble Arch. Yet much as I would have enjoyed seeing her, and welcomed the opportunity to relax for the first time in days, my conscience rebelled at simply turning up without notice. Laura was not tied to me, and having neglected her recently I could hardly protest if someone else happened to be staying the night. Before joining the motorway I hesitated again, and was on the point of telephoning, but again held back, deciding that a rude awakening in the early hours in the hope of a night's free bed-and-board was a selfish test of any friend's affection. In the event I decided to get back to Ardley. I liked driving, especially when there was little traffic; the big Volvo coped with my physical handicap in its stride; and the familiarity of my own bed was a reassuring prospect. Even so I remained uncomfortable about Laura; one day she'd marry some rich admirer and I would lose her for good.

After five hours' restless sleep I regretted not having vetoed that conscience. It had been a long day, and the confrontation with Tarrant more of a nervous strain than I had at first realised. Instead of enabling me to wind down, the pleasant but rather monotonous drive had the effect of stimulating my brain so that I spent the sleepless early hours repeatedly going over every minute of the break-in and its outcome in agonisingly slow motion. I had reached an impasse. The likelihood that Tarrant was involved in something underhand, supported by his 'proposition', did not necessarily link him with the Lanier journal. I thought about the bribe dispassionately; it was almost an irrelevance — money was not, in any case, something that interested me unduly, but what would he do if after a few days I had not responded either way. At breakfast — coffee and fresh grapefruit juice was all I could manage — I was still preoccupied. I doubted whether Tarrant would stick his neck out again in case I really had confided in the police: on the other hand *I* had no grounds for continuing to harass *him*.

Charlotte Hesse was another matter, but where would I start? Eventually common sense prevailed. I could not allow my 'conscience' — if that wasn't really an excuse for an inability to mind my own business — to dictate the way I ran my life. I had come to Ardley to develop a business, and even with Charlie Appleton on hand, there was more than enough to do. At that moment I decided to stop playing detectives.

Charlie fussed over my broken hand like a mother hen, but now I could set his mind to rest. I told him most of what had happened, and of my decision to put all that behind me and concentrate on the shop. He had seen me the worse for wear on other occasions, but could not get used to the idea of responsible adults behaving like belligerent delinquents, and his face brightened at the news. "Good! It's about time I was left to enjoy my retirement in peace."

"*Now* he tells me," I complained to the ceiling. "I only did it for him!"

"For me?" Charlie enquired.

"I thought you were bored so I created a little fantasy world crammed with adventure and excitement."

He pointed to my hand in plaster. "You needn't have gone to all that trouble just for me."

I shrugged. "It's not really broken — amazing what you can do with these junior doctor sets."

Although he smiled, he was not reassured, and when I announced that I was going to call on the Reverend Bill Darling, the new vicar of St Athelbert's Parish church, he insisted that I left the car behind because he did not 'hold' with one-handed drivers. The way I allowed Charlie to order me about was, I suppose, a sign of approaching maturity.

I go to church for weddings and funerals, although (if you'll pardon the expression) some of my best friends are clergymen, bibliophiles of one persuasion or another. The shop had been one of the Rev. Darling's first ports of call when he arrived in the town about three months earlier, and the acquaintanceship had developed to the point where we were now friends. Unlike his predecessor with whom I was merely on nodding terms, Darling seemed to be obsessed with books. The breadth of his literary interests made him an interesting and, more significantly, a compassionate man — although I am prepared to concede that I may be just a little biased. Like so many clergymen I know he seemed to spend more on books than he could afford, and I found myself cutting profit margins to indulge a fellow bibliophile. But the previous week Darling had left a message announcing the discovery of several hundred books which he now wanted to sell on behalf of the church, and while I had no illusions about the type of books that turn up at church fêtes, I felt an obligation to investigate, especially as finding suitable material to replenish stock is a major headache for booksellers these days.

At the vicarage I was welcomed by a preoccupied Mrs Darling, an attractive but highly strung woman, so anxious that I should remove the eyesore that cluttered parts of her living-room and the large hallway, that she even failed to notice the plaster that encased my left hand. I suppose I should have been pleased since I had been so self-conscious about it, but the absence of any interest in anything except the tidiness of her home irritated me. Darling, of course, spotted the injury at once, but although he kept glancing at it he was too well mannered to raise the matter before me.

"Got trampled on at a book sale," I remarked. "Dangerous business these days."

He pulled a face. "Well, at least you won't have to fight anyone off for this lot!"

I followed his glance at the rows of books stacked high, and my heart sank — practically everything was damp-stained, and some even sported a bilious-looking coating of mildew. I turned back to him accusingly. "Who unearthed this little lot — the grave-digger?"

He grinned sheepishly, looking for a moment like a guilty schoolboy. I estimated Darling was in his late forties, and the receding hairline and aura of dignity that comes with a vicar's rôle in the community made him seem older, yet his skin was unlined, and when he smiled one was reminded that initial impressions can be deceptive. "My call was a little premature," he admitted. "I got excited when I first saw them because those most accessible — that is, those nearest me — did not look so dilapidated. I didn't look behind them."

His wife made no comment but raised her eyes ostentatiously to Heaven. I disliked her instinctively, and suspected she nagged him unmercifully when they were alone. Now she favoured me with an expression of gentle resignation. "They are obviously of no use to you, Mr Coll. I think someone should call the Health Inspector before we all catch some terrible disease."

Disappointed though I was, I hurried to my friend's defence on principle. "Most of them can be dried out and tarted up — especially those with the leather bindings. Probably only surface damage in the main. Where on earth have they been kept?"

"Would you believe the steeple loft?" Darling asked, although from the disgust on his face it was not intended as a question. "When I arrived my predecessor, John Brangwyn, told me the steeple roof was leaking. It was mentioned almost in passing, and since the loft seemed to be dry I didn't think it could be that bad. There was so much else that needed urgent attention I put it out of my mind until I could find the time to take a proper look. It was only when we took up Brangwyn's huge tarpaulin that we found the books — providing a barrier against the elements, having effectively done what he considered they were best suited for. The man is a philistine."

As a book-lover the picture appalled but did not surprise me. I had even heard of a titled person who had used the family library to divert a river on his estate. I looked at the books dispassionately, finding them a strange assortment — some typical jumble-sale material, others much older and probably the property of an earlier incumbent. Several of the leather bindings I picked up were books about Dorset and on country sports, published in the 18th century. A few, with illustrations, were worth between £50 and £75 if they could be cleaned up.

I came to a quick decision. "Look, I can't do anything now, not with one good hand. Let's leave them where they are." I was conscious of Mrs Darling's theatrical despair, and rubbed it in. "Yes, just leave them there — I've got even less space than you." I waited until she could not contain her irritation any longer and repeated her suggestion of calling in the local council, before continuing as though I had not been interrupted. "You don't want to throw away £300 to £400!" I turned to him. "Bill, you don't need me to identify the dozen or so that are worth a bit — don't let's worry at this stage about *how* much — and I'll show you how to revive them, at least to some extent. Then we can see what they will fetch at auction. The rest are no use to anyone so why not have a jumble sale and offer the lot at 5p each, or in bargain boxes?"

"Excellent," he concurred, "but why don't you take the better ones for the shop."

"You'll get more at Crewkerne — but I'll cover your reserve price, so you won't lose either way."

He was embarrassed. "I can't let you do that, Matt. You've got a living to earn."

I shrugged. "You can do me a favour one of these days — or call it my donation to the steeple Restoration Fund; you'll need one."

86

He thanked me and I felt good. This is what running a country bookshop should be about — not only spending one's time pleasantly with books, but making a tangible contribution to the community. It was not about risking life and limb to find out whether people like Tarrant, living in another world, was dishonest — when no one else cared a damn. From now on I would know where my priorities lay.

On the stroll back I went over my plans for reorganising the shelves around the shop's fireplace, and wondering whether to tell Charlie I would not be needing him much longer. But when I arrived the enthusiasm was extinguished in one fell swoop by the news that Tom Duncan had phoned from London and was on his way down to see me.

My instinctive scowl was misinterpreted by Charlie. "How was I to know you didn't want to see him? He said he was in England for a week as the start of a European tour and was coming down to see you and do some buying. I thought you would be delighted."

I smiled at his confusion. "As an ambitious young bookseller I should be; he won't go away empty-handed. As an individual, I've decided I don't particularly like the man. He's too ruthless for my taste."

"You can be pretty single-minded yourself," Charlie pointed out.

I shrugged. "At least I can switch off. With Tom Duncan business always comes first; he makes no distinction between friend and enemy. Forget it, Charlie — just wearing my pride on my sleeve."

But I could not forget it; the feeling of contentment, or smugness, had evaporated. I was conscious of the butterflies in hibernation in my stomach starting to stir. What did Tom Duncan want with me? He could buy most of the books he needed without stirring from London, or at towns like Oxford within a 50-mile radius. He did not strike me as being the sort of man to travel more than 100 miles to one shop just to be sociable. He had told Charlie he was coming by train which meant I had to pick him up at Ardley station; so much for my plans for replanning the shelves.

When Duncan emerged from the train, I did not know whether to be relieved or suspicious at the big grin and warm handshake, and wondered whether I was developing a complex. We had spoken on the phone frequently. I had only met him once before and had forgotten what a good-looking man he was. About the same height and build as me, he had an open, honest face with steady blue eyes, even features, and a rather old-fashioned, crew-cut hairstyle. Despite a little excess weight around the shoulders and stomach, his clothes were a good fit. With his well-cut navy blue jacket, and light check gaberdines, and a very un-British tan he looked more like a Hollywood film star than a college librarian.

The show was obviously intended to be disarming, although he nearly went over the top, breaking off in mid-handshake to hold up a placatory palm. "Golly, I forgot," he exclaimed, with a pained expression. "I've got to apologise before you lay one on me?" He noticed my left hand. "I see you've been practising. Did he have a hard head, or did you just forget to close your fist?"

I had the feeling that if I had told him the truth about my investigation he would have the first train back to London. It was not so much that I was scared of his reaction, but that I wanted to discover the reason for his visit to Ardley; the best way was to let him call the tune for the time being. "Something like that," I said, picking up his overnight case in my good hand, and leading the way to my hired Volvo. "The only live entertainment in town is the bookshop — but I can recommend it," I said, doing the courier act with false bonhomie.

"Real books? With *words*?"

"I don't know — never looked inside the covers."

I despised the hypocrisy, but thankfully when we got to the shop there was no need to continue the act. Duncan was so impressed that the fixed smile disappeared by degrees as his professionalism took over. Partly because of my own interest in the subject and period I had a large section of scholarly books on 16th- and 17th-century literature, and when I drew it to his attention he seemed to go into a trance, removing titles in rapid succession until he had creamed off the best. Then he moved on to browse through the rest of the shop in such a relaxed manner that I was able to leave him and attend to other matters that required my attention. As he searched through the shelves he told me about his plans for the next few weeks, taking in Italy, France and Germany before ending up at an important book-fair in Holland. Typical of Duncan's single-mindedness was the decision to leave his wife behind; this was not a holiday — he was here to 'work'. From time to time he added to the pile of books he had assembled until eventually it was closing-time, and he had run up a bill of over $700.

The hours had passed pleasantly, and profitably for me, and it was not until we had sat down to dinner at Ardley's only Italian restaurant that Duncan finally came to the point. The menu at Luciano's is the sort that requires one's full attention — intimidating to the indecisive and daunting even to the gourmet who can still be made to feel he has been hurried into the wrong choice — yet just on the point of reaching a decision, he remarked, almost as an aside, "Let's talk about the journal."

"Why not?" I hedged.

He put the menu down and fixed me with those earnest blue eyes. "I want you to know, Matt, that despite the impression my reaction on the phone must have given, I took what you had to say very seriously. You have to understand that while I respect your judgement, I also respect the judgement of most of my colleagues, and *we* quarrel all the time!" He broke off to laugh, as though demonstrating that he was conscious of his own shortcomings. "Anyway, for the sake of the library I refused to continue on the assumption of my infallibility. We have some talented people at the university, so I decided to make use of the services of a couple — neither of whom knew anything about Emilia Lanier; in fact, I doubt whether one of them had even heard of her."

I grunted in a non-committal voice, giving my attention to the soup that had been placed in front of me, and Duncan continued. "As far as I'm concerned, their input confirms my stand, but I thought it would set your mind at rest too . . . " From an inside breast-pocket he produced and handed to me two sheets of folded paper. I identified them as photostats of a couple of pages from the journal, although it was not a section I remembered. "This is from the year 1592," he explained. "I'd like you to read it so that we can discuss certain factors in the light of my new information." He applied himself

to the food so that I could concentrate on the journal.
As I began, the empathy with Emilia Lanier came flooding back:

23rd September

Will there bee no end to my humilyation. I am with Childe, but the man who robb'd me of my virtve hath willd that I mvst for colour become the spovvse of another vvithin the moneth. The VVorlde shal knowe my Husbande marryes me for his preferrment & the annuitie of Forty Pounds which it seemeth is all I am worthe. Hunsdon is the onlie man who hath knowne me these past yeares but now hee treateth me as a Harlot.

I am inform'd my Husbande is a worthie servant to the Queens Majestie, from which I foreseeth hee is ready to complie with my Lords vvishes. Lanyer, for that is his name, wil bee offered a commission abroad so I will bee free to entertain my old frends, by which Hunsdon meaneth himself. This uile old man hath rvined me, and when my bellie bee swollen vvonderfull large euen his serpant Lust will vvither.

If my Father had lived I would not Today bee the plaething of a rich old mizer, or next moneth the svffering wife of a young man that bee poor. If I was not with childe I would seek a more worthie protector. Wouldst that I could bee certaine of my onne trve loue, that he respect'd my virtve as much as my beautie. Thou hath talk'd of Marriage, svveet Henry, but how can I bee certaine it was not in ieste. Does thou knowe how much thou excites me? Does thou knowe my hawtie manner is an act worthie of the playhouse, that in truethe I melte at thy touch? I would bee thy spowse tomorrowe if thou would but ask. But I am a fool & my misfortvn is a ivste revvard. Southampton will not marrye me. Hee is ambitiovs & shal not endanger his position at Covrte by consorting openly with a Commoner. If hee desireth me at all, it is not for my intelligense.

Why am I neuer satisfied, alvvays at odds with the VVorlde? In truethe my loue for Southampton is an ilvsion. Why must I denie euen to myself that my passion is fiered by his indifference, vvhile I haue onlie contempt for those who throwe themselves at my feet? His companion of all houres the actor Shakespear pleases him mightily, yet it is a frendship I cannot vnderstand. The fellow is a red-faced cuntry bvmkin when hee speaketh to me; the straw stil trapping his tung. For all his flovvering repvtation as a playright, it is said hee is meerely an actor who hath learn'd the trade from others & who hath an ear for the prettie frase. My thoghts are of little conseqvence, but hee is sorely ivdged by his Peers. I have seene printed this moneth a letter Robert Greene hath writ before his Death. Shakespear be a strvtting peecock (quoth hee).

I know not why I strayne my eyes scribbling about the fellowe; yet there must bee some qualitie in a man so ful of contradictions. I wonder that one so tung-tyed in my presence can pen svch vvittie uerse, vnless he is inspierdt by others of better birth . . . but Henry wil not agree & sweares the man doth posses gifts the VVorlde hath not yet seene. I must not scorne him for I svspect the stuttering Will loveth mee, & Mistris

Lanyer can no longer afforde the Bassano pride.

Svveet God, grant that one day I shal bee indepcndent of rich men, that I bee respect'd as a person of qualitie, of intelligense and vvitte, not meerely of Beautie.

When I looked up again, moved by Emilia's passion, my solemn expression brought a half-smile to his face, although this time I could see he was sincere. "We're *all* just a little in love with her," he reflected. "But I selected that passage because in just over 500 words, it is Emilia who shoots down all the hot-air talked about a forgery." He quickly dismissed the doubts that still showed in my face. "*Not* in any emotional sense; we've approached this clinically."

I shrugged. "I'm prepared to meet you more than half-way."

"An open mind is all I ask," he replied. "I started with a handwriting expert. I'll admit I'm not 100 per cent sold on them as a breed, but a lot of people are, and they are accepted these days in the courts. Besides, I imposed my own conditions on our man, Chuck Danvers. I didn't show him the diary — only some photostats, shuffled out of sequence. I didn't want him to be influenced in any way by the content." I nodded in agreement, and he smiled rather smugly. "He didn't need any help. He just browsed through the pages for two or three minutes — and remember some of that time was needed to familiarise himself with the period lettering, and some of her inconsistencies in spelling — and then came up with a barrage of conclusions right off the top of his head, one after the other in quick succession."

"And?" I prompted, urging him to get to the point.

"He said it was a woman's handwriting. He said

it was written under stress, probably in secret. Then he became more aware of the *dates* of the entries, realised it was a diary, and apologised for stating the obvious. He went on to say she was a person of strong personality, being very much a loner — intelligent, highly sensitive, bitter."

"We knew that," I interrupted.

"From *reading* the journal. He was merely analysing handwriting he had never seen before, penned by a person about whom he had no prior knowledge."

"What was his reaction to the forgery theory?"

"Unfortunately he was not prepared to take up the challenge unless we could produce another sample of Emilia Lanier's handwriting with which to compare it. So in *this* instance all our expert established was that it was written by a woman — not necessarily Emilia."

I was relieved to see that he was at least prepared to make some concession, and nodded contentedly. "I'll go along with that."

He grinned at my caution. "I'm not saying that proves anything, but the law of averages and precedent must count for something: how many women forgers spring to mind?"

I could not think of any.

His smile broadened. "I wouldn't stake my reputation on it, but I did take the trouble to do a little digging, and I couldn't find one either. There were forgers I had forgotten about, and forgers I'd never *heard* of before — but not one female. I won't labour the point. Next, I took the genuine article to Bob Priestley, head of our school of psychology. I asked him as a special favour to spend an evening with the journal as though the author was one of his case histories. I told him nothing about Emilia apart from a few sparse facts about her background and English society in the late 16th century.

"Next day he provided me with a report that indicated he already knew her as well as me or the research team which had spent *weeks* with her. He diagnosed a woman frustrated by her environment; the strait-jacket imposed on her by her looks and the times in which she lived."

"Does it need a psychologist to recognise that?" I interrupted.

"It goes to recognise *behaviour* characteristics; for example, her inconsistency — not just in spelling. She objects to being treated as a mistress and yet in the same breath talks of finding a 'more worthie' protector, which means there was no urgent desire to change the status — only the partner. That, and a dozen other examples he describes as standard behaviour patterns, but you know these guys — the way they duck behind a smoke-screen of technical jargon? I forced him to come off his high horse and to speculate whether the journal could have been a forgery — on the assumption that it's value depended on two important ingredients: the references to Shakespeare, and the strong implication of 16th-century 'woman's lib'.

"Like Chuck, he was reluctant at first to express an opinion, except to suggest that a forger might more blatantly have given his public what it wanted; in other words, a reference to the Bard on every page and, of course, all the intimate details of their sex life.

"Again we didn't need him to tell us that. So I fed him one or two bits of information about Emilia, for example, read him some of the poetry that was published nearly twenty years later. When he realised how good the material was, he suggested that a forger setting out to push the woman's lib point of view would have made more of her unquestioned talent. Yet in the whole diary there is no evidence that she tried to influence Hunsdon in his dealings with the theatre companies, or Shakespeare, or anyone else for that matter. And the reason can only be that the real Emilia knew that such interference would not be tolerated. From an intelligent *wife*, perhaps, but not from a mistress — a state of affairs that is hard for the modern mind to accept."

I shrugged. "Makes sense. But getting into the period is not beyond the talented forger. You've quoted two experts who merely confirm the unlikelihood of the journal having been forged — not proved it to be genuine."

Duncan retained his good humour. "I don't have to *prove* anything. If the issue ever arose, the onus would be on proving the opposite. But I said I came to convince you, and I haven't finished yet. The last and most impressive point is something the research team spotted. Emilia quotes the writer Robert Greene to make her point about Shakespeare being overrated."

He leaned over and indicated the relevant passage with a finger. "See: '. . . a strutting peecock'. Well, Greene never said anything of the sort. He was pretty nasty about Shakespeare — Marlowe and Nashe too for that matter — although to be fair he didn't know it was going to be published, but the phrase he used was from his *A Groats Worth of Wit*. It's quite well known; doesn't it ring a bell?" I shook my head, and he continued: "The correct passage read: '. . . an *upstart crow* beautiful with our feathers'. Dissipated bastard; he was an absolute wreck when he died, though he was only about five years older than

Shakespeare."

"Now you come to mention it, the 'upstart crow' bit is familiar, but I didn't get the connection before."

"Exactly. Greene is better known today for that crack than he is for his creative writing, which is a pity. Shouldn't have been such a jealous sod. But to get back to us: a forger trying to be so accurate in every other respect would have *checked*. I knew the passage but I still looked it up again because the rest of the piece was just as interesting. Greene went on a bit about Shakespeare — although, of course, he didn't actually name anyone. What he said was, and I quote: '. . . with his tygers hart wrapt in a Players hyde*, supposes he is well able to bombast out a blanke verse as the best of you; and being an absolute Johannes fac totum*, is in his owne conceit the only Shake-scene in a country!' "

Duncan looked at me challengingly, but I did not react, and he concluded triumphantly. "No, Emilia must have read Greene's tract; she was probably part of that Bohemian circle, but relied on her memory — as one would in a personal diary where accuracy is not a consideration — for what *she* regarded as an endorsement of her conviction that Will was simply too big for his boots."

I could visualise Emilia's anguish as she poured out her heart to the only intimate confidante she had — her journal — and his theory rang true. I conceded the point and he sighed expansively.

"Great. Believe it or not, Matt, you're the only person whose opinion matters to me. I could not rest while there was any doubt still nagging at your conscience — and mine."

I was flattered and tried to respond by being equally frank. "You seemed to interpret my misgivings as a personal attack on your integrity. It wasn't like that. My persistence was only a sense of obligation to you and the university."

He nodded amiably, almost it seemed with affection. "I know that, Matt, which is why I went to all this trouble to demonstrate that it was not just a question of old big-head here standing on his dignity."

I could not help responding to the mood of frankness, and if he had left the matter there, our relationship would have been fused by a new and stronger bond of trust and comradeship. But Tom Duncan did not like 'loose-ends', and his single-mindedness spoilt all that effort. I had signalled to the waiter for our bill when Duncan, seeking to capitalise on the new intimacy, caught my eye and proposed quite formally as though we were in a committee meeting that the subject be closed. Not only was the question posed in that way, but he sat back and waited for an answer.

I hesitated. "Closed? If you're referring to the suggestion of a lab test, I had already conceded it was your decision, not mine." I smiled in what I hoped was a disarming manner, and added, "I'll stop *nagging* you, if that's what you mean."

He made a slightly dismissive gesture with his head to indicate that was only part of what he meant. "Nagging doesn't really worry me, I suppose; I've got a thick skin. It's the ripples you've been creating in an otherwise still pond — asking around about this and that."

The insinuation intrigued me. "How did *you* know I had made enquiries?"

He shrugged. "You forget I have a lot of contacts and friends in this country. At that stage I believe you were acting in our best interests, but after what you've heard today those interests are best

98

served by letting the matter drop. I'd feel happier with an assurance."

The knot of irritation in my stomach began to fester. If I had been able to lose my temper and release the tension the inflammation might have died down, but the effort of remaining calm exacerbated the discomfort. "As a matter of fact, Tom, I had decided to do just that — *before* you came today, but I don't know what you mean by my 'assurance'? You've got no more right to demand that than I have to insist on the lab tests. I believe, because I want to believe, that the journal is genuine — but I'll never be convinced beyond the proverbial 'shadow of doubt' until that paper and ink have been analysed."

I could see that he was also struggling to control his temper. "That's your prerogative, Matt. Believe what you will, but meanwhile *I* don't want people gossiping because of *your* irresponsible enquiries. It's always assumed there is no smoke without a fire."

"The same people might wonder why you're trying so hard to stop me."

"I should have thought that was obvious."

I stood up. "You've made your point. If you can't trust my judgement there's nothing more to say. If you want to catch the next train to London, we had better leave now."

At the station we both made an effort to remain civil, but the strain between us had returned. Duncan was a man who did not like his authority challenged, while no one could coerce me in a month of Sundays into doing something that went against the grain.

I had a sleepless night. The aggravation had given me indigestion, which in turn kept me awake, and inevitably I kept turning over in my mind the discussion at dinner. There was no question that Tom Duncan believed in the journal, and I shared that belief, except for — no, I *did* believe in it. Then why could I not leave well alone? I assured myself with a snigger: "Because it's there," like a mountain waiting to be climbed, but also because other people — Tarrant and Tom Duncan in their different ways had gone to extremes — *wanted* me to stop.

Duncan had persuaded me that the manuscript had been written by a woman — and if it had not been Emilia Lanier, then she had to be a person of intelligence, possessing an empathy for the woman who had inspired it. Charlotte Hesse was again the likeliest candidate, and I had to find a way to link them.

SIX

That night before dozing off fitfully I made another resolution — to do something about my health. The indigestion was a timely reminder that I was eating too much, and the wrong foods. I knew instinctively from the way I constantly averted my eyes from the bathroom scales that I was probably about 20 pounds overweight. It was also reflected in how easily I got out of breath and the dizziness I experienced after squatting down to get at books on the lower shelves. The problem with athletic persons of my endomorph build is that we have a tendency to gain weight in unadulterated flab as soon as we stop exercising, so a special effort was needed.

Even in my drugged state after seven restless hours, the incentive to get fit again was strong enough to get me into my track-suit and jog for about three miles before taking a cold shower. I felt so good that the halo distinctly visible two inches above my head enabled me to resist the temptation of a bacon and egg breakfast, and settle for a half-grapefruit — without sugar. Then with chest out and stomach pulled in I planned my day: the book department at Chesterton's, the auction-house where Charlotte

Hesse seemed to be so well known that she had the run of the place; the reading-room at the British Library where I hoped to examine Emilia Lanier's book of poems *Salve Deus Rex Judaeorum* for inspection, and finally a pleasant evening with Laura Cottingham.

I rang Laura first to 'reserve' her — and a bed — for the night; and then made an appointment with Jonathon Harker, head of the manuscript department at Chesterton's. With my new-found energy I even telephoned Mr Bereton to apologise for the delay in returning his clothes, and the police at Wells who agreed for the sake of convenience all round to allow me to make my full statement to Ardley police, where I was on friendly terms with Detective Inspector Murdoch.

I took the train to London, partly to appease Charlie Appleton, and partly because these days I dreaded the city's day-time parking headaches. There was no book or manuscript sale at the auction-house, and Harker was polite enough to pretend that he had nothing more important to do than entertain me over coffee. He was an aesthetic man in his middle fifties; a trace of superciliousness about him, but friendly in a businesslike way. We had met only once — when I had bought the Lanier — but I suppose that association and the possibility that I might repeat the pattern in some future sale was incentive enough. We began with the customary small talk — he had a small fund of amusing anecdotes about the trade, but when I narrowed the field to Charlotte Hesse the gossip seeemed to dry up.

Although my opening question had been innocuous enough, and his reaction — "Charming girl!" — appeared to be spontaneous, he proceeded to re-

102

verse our rôles by suddenly asking about my interest in her. "Or shouldn't I enquire?" he added rather coyly.

I did my best to blush, and confided that the enquiry was off-the-record. "I was thinking of using her as a writer and researcher for an historical biography I intend to publish. I thought you might be able to give an independent assessment of her abilities."

He nodded agreeably. "Couldn't find a better person. We have always been most impressed with her knowledge."

"Does she have any academic training?"

"I should *think* so, but I really don't know. In all the years I've known her Charlotte has never volunteered information about herself. On the contrary, she seems to have thrown down a challenge to us all: take me as you find me — strictly on merit."

I did not prolong the discussion with Harker; not interested in joining the Charlotte Hesse fan club.

With that line of enquiry closed, the only avenue still open was Emilia Lanier. I wondered if there was come clue in her poetry. At the British Library I managed to get myself a temporary reading-room ticket by claiming that I was carrying out research into the work of 17th-century women poets. The library's copy of *Salve Deus Rex Judaeorum* was one of only two or three copies known to exist, and holding the thin pocket-size volume for the first time brought back the emotional impact of having the journal to myself for that brief period. I opened it almost reverently. The title page read as follows, although for convenience I have modernised the type faces and altered the lay-out slightly:

SALVE DEUS REX JUDAEORUM

Containing

1 The Passion of Christ
2 Eves Apologie in defence of Women
3 The Teares of the Daughters of Jerusalem
4 The Salutation and Sorrow of the Virgin Mary

With divers other things not unfit to be read

Written by Mistress Æmilia Lanyer, Wife to Captain Alfonso Lanyer Servant to the Kings Majestie

AT LONDON

Printed by Valentine Simmes for Richard Bonian, and are to be sold at his Shop in Paules Churchyard, at the Sogne of the Floure de Luce and Crown, 1611

I browsed restlessly through the pages, wondering where to start, fascinated by the number of dedications to persons of rank, all women: the Queen Elizabeth, the Countesses of Bedford and Dorset, the Dowager Countess of Cumberland, and one section to 'all virtuous ladies in general'. The names meant very little to me, with the exception of the Countess of Cumberland, whom I recalled was the widow of one of the most swashbuckling men of his time — George Clifford, the third Earl, and most enthusiastic of Elizabethan privateers; an adventurer who would have given little thought or consideration to any wife. I studied the poem for some indication of Emilia's soured view of men, and soon discovered the following passage:

...Thou from the Court to the Country art retired,
Leaving the world, before the world leaves thee:
That great Enchantress of weak minds admired,
Whose all-bewitching charms so pleasing be
To wordly wantons; and too much desired
Of those that care not for Eternity:
But yield themselves as preys to Lust and Sin,
Losing their hopes of Heaven Hell pains to win ...

Then, after praising the Dowager Duchess's apparent preference for God over man, she went on to attack the priorities of a society that puts conventional beauty before virtue:

...As for those matchless colours Red and White,
Or perfect features in a fading face,
Or due proportion pleasing to the fight;
All these do draw but dangers and disgrace:
A mind enriched with Virtue, shines more bright,
Addes everlasting Beauty, gives true grace,
Frames an immortal Goddess on the earth,
Who though she dies, yet Fame gives her new berth.

That pride of Nature which adorns the fair,
Like blazing comets to allure all eyes,
Is but the thread that weaves their web of Care,
Who glories most where most their danger lies;
For greatest perils do attend the fair;
When men do seek, attempt, plot and devise,
How they may overthrow the chastest Dame,
Whose Beauty is the White whereat they aim ...

I had been mildly infatuated with Emilia Lanier, and while I could understand the resentment at being discarded by Hunsdon, and probably Southampton, her bitterness against men in general seemed out of proportion for such an intelligent woman. And then I remembered the *Sonnets,* which had been published only two years before her poems. Shakespeare's anguished but violent attack on his former mistress, written before the wounds had healed, must have been humiliating to Emilia — especially as it seems she had patronised him at the outset. I forced myself to stop that train of thought. There was no evidence of that, apart from the journal, and could I still trust the manuscript? What could not be disputed was that although no one at the time would have identified her with the Dark Lady in the *Sonnets* Emilia had alwys been hypersensitive, and now, the dream of the Court and artistic recognition faded, she would have felt especially vulnerable. Was this something that Charlotte Hesse could have guessed or felt?

I read on, finding some of the material embarrassingly sycophantic and damaging to my mental picture of Emilia. Her opinion of men, however, was riveting: '. . . to be practised by evil-disposed men, who — forgetting they were born of women, nourished of women and that if it were not by the means of women they would be quite extinguished out of the world and a final end of them all — do, like vipers, deface the wombs wherein they were bred. . . .'

I looked at my watch; two hours had passed in what secmed like minutes, and it was obviously impossible to finish some 80 sides of text before the library closed for the evening. I decided to photostat the contents so that I could examine them at my leisure, but at the enquiry desk I discovered that, because of its age and rarity, the little book came into a special category which it was not possible to photostat. I would need electrostatic prints which could not be done on the spot. Since I was staying the night in London I wondered if I could call back the following day, but I was not the only person making demands on the Library's photographic department; the backlog meant a delay of between seven and eight weeks. My frustration was evident, until the assistant added: "Unless we already have the negatives. . . ."

I leapt at the half-chance, and asked if it was possible to check immediately. I was passed on to an assistant who looked aghast at the prospect. "It's possible that a colleague of mine had some prints done about — " I reflected for a moment or two on the likeliest period, and took an educated gamble — between one year and two years ago. The person is abroad at present so I can't ask directly." The man's face did not change much, so I beguiled him with my most earnest expression. "It's *very* important for me to know. I'm going abroad myself tomorrow." To give him credit he went off to check the records with barely a grimace, and when he returned less than ten minutes later it was with a braod smile. He looked pleased with himself. I returned the smile. "Any luck?"

He nodded. "It could have taken hours, but I checked first to find out whether we had any negative at all. We did; made just over three months ago — so I cross-checked with the order-book for that date. We had one for a C. Hesse, presumably Mr. Is that him?"

I nodded. I could not understand why the date was so recent, but the name was good enough for me. "I'm much obliged to you — that's saved me a lot of money." I left contentedly, no longer concerned with studying the poems. The fact that

Charlotte Hesse had already been along the same route was significant. It *proved* nothing, but it confirmed a more than casual interest in a woman few people had even heard of until the publication of A. L. Rowse's fascinating study of Simon Forman, another lover of the Dark Lady.

I often wondered why Laura Cottingham put up with me. It's not a question of false modesty — but as puzzled friends would point out, Laura was something special. She had a sparkling personality that tended to overshadow the fact that she was also strikingly beautiful and enormously intelligent. There is no question that I loved her, but to be *in love*, in the starry-eyed 'panting' context has all the unpredictability of a secret chemical formula. Our relationship seemed to travel through time and space with tranquillity for most of the time, but was from time to time sucked into the 'black holes' which turn behaviour patterns inside-out. This meant that I felt 'tied' to her in everything but the legal sense, yet had occasionally fallen for other women, while she said nothing, never complained and always seemed to be there when I wanted to return. She was independent enough to lead her own life, and even to 'punish' me when I overstepped the mark, but I suppose I tend to complacency; if she had a serious affair I would have been as jealous as hell, but most of the time I knew I had nothing to worry about, despite the number of men laying siege at any one time. It was perhaps like being married but being kept apart by our work.

I was early enough to pick Laura up from the advertising agency where she was a main board director, although most of her time was still spent with the copy-writing team. She was obviously pleased to see me, kissed me warmly on the mouth, but then confessed that she could not leave until her unit had come up with a solution to a 'pay-off' line they could not get right. I was taken to the drinks cabinet in the boardroom and told to 'make myself at home'. A pretty young secretary came in with a plate of sandwiches, and even I was impressed with the agency's ability to rustle up food at a time of day when most of the staff were on the point of leaving. I had a rather patronising attitude to the advertising agency lifestyle, but could see why Laura valued her job, and would be loathe to leave it.

Fortified by the food and drink, I browsed through the bookcase, for once conscious of the time and unable to concentrate on the books. When I had taken over the shop at Ardley, Laura had come down for most week ends, but gradually — and it had coincided with the start of the bad weather during the winter — the visits had become infrequent. Now, having seen her for the first time in almost two months, I was overwhelmed by her vitality, wondering how I could have allowed the parting to be so lengthy. Most of her colleagues knew me, and as they popped in for a drink at different times I was conscious of the fact that the men in particular were somewhat antagonistic, presumably wondering why I did not let go of the traces — and leave her to worthier suitors. On occasions like that I shared their consternation.

By the time Laura returned it had gone seven o'clock, and I had lost my appetite, but, very conveniently, Laura claimed to be on a slimming diet, so we took in a film and returned to her flat for a lighter snack. The two-bedroom apartment in a luxury block three minutes' walk from Marble Arch was on a long lease and had been purchased with a small family inheritance, but the monthly rent was about twice my mortgage repayment, and her living-standards were sky-high compared with mine. Later, relaxed and purring with contentment we listened to Albinoni and Vivaldi on a stereo system that might have had me drooling with envy had it belonged to anyone else. I reflected on the times she had jokingly offered to 'save' me from becoming a country bumpkin; now she seemed to be content to leave matters as they were. The unpredictability of women in general made me think again of Emilia Lanier — and Charlotte, and I decided to get the benefit of a feminine perspective on the problem.

Earlier I had joked about the cause of my broken hand; now I gave her a full account of everything that happened to me. She listened, fascinated, without interruption until I had brought her up to date, and then broke in with a series of penetrating questions about the character of Emilia Lanier.

When I had finished, she went to the bookcase and produced a thick works of Shakespeare so that we could refresh our memories of the *Sonnets*. We read passages aloud to each other, at one stage her eyes filling with tears at the pain that had been exorcised in the writing. I was momentarily surprised at the reaction; obviously our sympathies were divided. When I mentioned it she laughed. "Only because you heard her side of the story first from the journal. To me she sounds like a frustrated bitch; my sympathies are with him, although if he suffered as much as it appears from the *Sonnets*, then we should be grateful to her. It was after their affair that he produced some of his most moving work. It's probably true that suffering moulds the character."

It was characteristic of my obsession with the authenticity of the journal, that I had never thought of Emilia being anything other than an exploited woman; the fact that there were two sides to any story had not occurred to me. I leaned over, kissed her gratefully and concluded: "Well, don't just sit there, take a few days off and find out whether the manuscript is a forgery or not. *I'm* not getting anywhere."

"What, and have your Mr Tarrant throw *me* into a vat of boiling paper?"

"It wasn't boiling, but in any case my Mr Tarrant would eat out of your hand. *You* would only have to *ask*, and he'd confess everything. Unfortunately, we've passed on to Charlotte Hesse, and she *doesn't* respond to charm."

"Why don't you let me have a go at her?"

"I'd like nothing better. I'm stuck for ideas — short of beating her over the head with a cricket bat."

"But even if you can come up with something more subtle, she's going to be suspicious of anyone associated with me. Frensham, bless him, mentioned your name when we were introduced."

Laura's face lit up; she was impressed by Frensham's old-world charm and sophistication. "Why would he do that?"

Her eyes, wide with mock innocence, teased me, and I could not help rising to the bait. "Just being polite, in the way that one asks after — an elderly relative, for example."

She refused to react in the way I had expected. "Then there's no reason for her to remember the name?"

"I suppose not."

111

"Are you sure he didn't mention my eyes? Wilfred is very taken with my eyes — something to do with the colour green and my auburn hair. He keeps on and on about it. Now if he mentioned *that* to another woman she wouldn't forget."

I was forced to throw in the towel. "No, it was me who mentioned them. She kept fluttering *her* eyelashes at me, and I had to tell her she was wasting her time, and that I was hooked on Laura Cottingham who has the most beautiful eyes in the world."

"Darling," she echoed.

"And *that* was when Frensham said 'Laura *who*?' "

She leaned over and kissed me. "If he's going to play hard to get, I'll have to settle for you."

I returned the kiss, quickly losing interest in Charlotte Hesse, but Laura pulled away and added, "There is no reason for her to connect us. I can arrange some sort of introduction through our media department. I'm sure one of our people is on friendly terms with her advertising department — after all, they carry quite a few of our ads."

I nodded. The idea appealed to me. "Your officer is much appreciated," I told her.

"Don't mention it. She sounds an interesting person, and I have to have some social life. Most of the men who hang around are a drag — present company excepted, and you're *never* around — so if she's pleasant company there's no problem. Nevertheless, gaining the confidence of someone who seems to be somewhat introverted can't be done overnight."

"Obviously. But if anyone can break down those barriers, I'm sure it's you."

She smiled. "Meanwhile, you'll *have* to stay in

112

touch now if you want up-to-date progress reports."

I got to my feet and pulled her up. "Talking about progress reports, I haven't put you through your paces recently."

"I thought you'd never ask," she said, heading for the bedroom.

SEVEN

With confidence in Laura's ability to infiltrate the
barriers that isolated and protected Charlotte Hesse,
I was able to return to Ardley and concentrate on
broadening the investigation begun on the premise
that Tarrant and van der Meeran had been collabora-
tors who had fallen out. But where did Charlotte
fit into that relationship? There was, of course, the
possibility I had confused their rôles — that the ball
had been served from the Dutchman's court. Yet my
image of van der Meeran supported the theory that
he had been an accessory *after* the fact; in which
case how had they gone about recruiting him?
Tarrant, for example, would have had greater opportunity; he travelled to the Continent from time to
time on business, and to attend trade exhibitions.

The question was too open-ended. I focused my
attention on Tarrant; we had not been in touch since
the night of my break-in, and it seemed unlikely
that he would try to contact me now — a negative
situation that could only work to my detriment.
As long as I maintained some sort of dialogue there
was a possibility that I might unearth another, more
encouraging lead. Tarrant would be suspicious, but

I had nothing to lose, providing I did not underestimate him again. Over the next 24 hours I mentally rehearsed that telephone conversation, anticipating every permutation of response.

When I was on the point of putting it to the test, a snippet of news from Laura lifted my spirits. Slipping into what she considered the appropriate jargon she reported she had made contact with the 'target' at the press preview of an art exhibition to which she had been invited by the advertising manager of Charlotte's paper, the *Morning Herald*. "I got my media people to introduce me to this guy, Paul Davenport, over a drink in Fleet Street. Believe it or not, I persuaded him I was art groupie, or whatever they call themselves; said I would do *anything* to get to the Tate preview. No sweat to a fixer like Paul. At the show I got him to introduce me to the target — to whom I declared, hand on heart, that her column was the first feature to which I turned at breakfast — which was true, at least since I took on the assignment. Then I twisted his arm to take us both to lunch."

"Poor sod. I bet he didn't know what hit him."

"Oh, he wasn't as shell-shocked as all that. Despite his smooth talk Paul's a pretty cold-blooded operator. He has a mind like a one-armed bandit; gives *nothing* away. He would have looked me over and converted my moving parts into the type of vital statistics he feeds that mechanical brain of his. He wouldn't have pulled the handle unless he could see stars lined up and reckoned he was going to hit the jackpot."

I found the cheerfulness in her voice slightly disquieting. "For a famous copywriter, you seem to trip over your metaphors very clumsily," I joked, but with an edge to my voice.

Laura was riding high and kicked me as I was going down. "Well, he *is* very experienced in those matters. I'm not too sure I can handle him."

"You mean when he pointed out that three was a crowd you decided not to bother taking his boring arts correspondent?"

"You guessed!"

"Get on with your report, 008," I commanded.

She laughed. "As a matter of fact, *Charlotte* wasn't very keen. I don't think she likes the smooth type."

"An Arts correspondent has to have good taste," I interjected.

"When Paul was getting us some champagne, I hinted that *I* didn't want to have lunch with him alone, and that by joining us she would be saving me from a fate worse than death."

I managed to bite back a jealous retort. "And did she?"

"Yes. I'm glad to say — quite apart from what I had set out to do. We hit it off immediately. I like her and I think she likes me — at least, she had promised to take me to another press show next week."

"Well done!"

She sighed. "I'm already having qualms. When I volunteered it seemed like an exciting undercover job. Now that I've met and like the girl, I feel I'm betraying her trust."

"At least give it a whirl. If I'm right there'll be no need to waste any tears. Meanwhile, I trust you've dispensed with the services of that smarmy go-between. You're too young to lose your virginity to a creep like that."

She laughed. "My virginity is still in peril; I agreed

116

to have dinner with him on Friday." She seemed to hesitate before adding: "He did do me a favour, and I couldn't be rude, especially in a semi-business situation between the agency and his paper.

I could not tell whether she was still teasing, or merely trying to be honest, but I had to curb my jealousy until I was prepared to do something constructive about our relationship, so I took a deep breath and offered my congratulations on the progress made.

With the news still fresh in my mind I decided to try my luck on the phone with Tarrant. Although his manner was less confident than before, the tone was guarded. "That — er — proposition you put to me the other night," I began, "you can save your money."

A shade of hostility coloured his tone. "What does that mean? I still have to keep looking over my shoulder?"

"I would hardly telephone to put you on your guard," I said. "On the contrary, you can relax. My client in the States, like so many institutional bodies, is frightened to death of any kind of scandal. Words like 'forgery' and 'fake' are anathema to them. Since *they* are 100 per cent satisfied the journal is authentic, they've asked me to drop my enquiry *forthwith.*"

There was a pregnant silence, as though Tarrant could not decide whether I was the bringer of good news, or preparing a trap. Eventually he gave a nervous laugh, and said, "I told you all along you were wasting your time."

"*Relax!* I haven't tapped your phone, so don't insult my intelligence by trying to pretend you're a law-abiding citizen. Whatever you've been up to must have been illegal, but it's no longer any of my business. My main reason for calling was to save you the bother."

"Of what?"

"Of trying to kill me all over again."

My provocative tone unsettled him, and he sniggered again. "Not everyone would appreciate your sense of humour, Mr Coll. Is there something else on your mind?"

"No. I think I've made it clear enough. From now on, don't call me — and I won't call you."

As I had planned my show of indifference had the effect of dispelling his fear of a trap, and he took the bait at last. "Hang on a minute," he called out. "Look, I understand how you feel, but why don't we let bygones be bygones? I want to make it up to you for the *suit* at least; as a peace-offering why don't I come and look at your stock. Despite your preoccupation the other night you couldn't have helped noticing I'm a serious collector?"

I maintained the act. "I'm in business to sell books. If you want to buy, I can hardly turn you away."

"Good," he responded with enthusiasm. Although I could not be certain why he had reacted in this way, I was reasonably confident it was motivated by curiosity. His pride would also have been hurt; we had clashed head-on like prize bulls and 'honours', if that was the right word, could be called even. Now he was being dismissed as unimportant, and he objected to it. Human nature is such that he pursued me now for much the same reason as he would have retreated had I continued to display an interest. Now *he* wanted to know just how much *I* knew.

"There is always someone here," I pointed out,

118

"but if you want to see me just ring the day before to make sure."

He promised to do that, and after a momentary hesitation added, "We might find we have something in common — *apart* from cuts and bruises. I'm looking forward to it."

"At least *we* seem to know where we stand. I wish your friend Charlotte Hesse was as sensible."

"How do you mean?"

"*Something* is going on. Wish I could tell you," I said mysteriously, and put the phone down.

I was not given long to enjoy my bathe in the smug glow of catching Tarrant off-balance, being brought down to earth by a phone call from Jonathon Harker of Chesterton's. "Have you had any further thoughts about commissioning that book from Charlotte Hesse?"

"Not yet," I stalled.

"Well, it's an incredible coincidence that you should have mentioned her because only a few days later who do you think walked in out of the blue?"

I took a stab at the obvious, and he continued delightedly, "Even more remarkable she has been coming to see us for years as a journalist — you might say as an *observer*; now she has joined the club."

"How do you mean?"

"Become a *vender.*"

"Oh?"

"Which is why I telephoned. May I speak to you strictly off the record?"

"Of course."

"What she has to offer is in monetary terms nothing really remarkable — worth about £2,000 I suppose. She is interested in a quick sale, and since she has been a good friend to Chesterton's — you can imagine how important it is for us to keep the press sweet — we agreed that she would probably do better by selling direct if she could find the right buyer. I thought of you because I believe you did say that your client — the American library — had a special interest in the Tudor and Stuart periods. Well, this is only an autograph *letter*, but it has an important connection with the Restoration theatre. I'm sure they would give their eyeteeth for an item like this."

I was flummoxed. Did Harker's fellow directors know what was going on? Turning away business merely to keep a journalist 'sweet'? Yet Chesterton's were a law unto themselves — large and successful enough to break the rules if it suited them. I was conscious of Harker hanging on to the phone with remarkable patience. "Sorry to be so indecisive," I apologised. "It sounds too good to be true — of course, I'll speak to my client. What are the details?"

"I've got them written down here, although naturally you would need to come to inspect the item before taking any decision. Meanwhile, since we're dealing with a single-page letter there isn't very much to tell. Have you heard of a man called Sir Henry Herbert; had the title 'Master of the Revels'?"

I admitted I had not.

"Well, fortunately there is a wealth of material about him in most theatre histories. I have in front of me Allardyce Nicoll's *A History of English Drama 1660-1900,* and I can read you what he says:

> Herbert, who had been appointed Master of the Revels in 1623 and through whose skilled management that post had been turned into a

most lucrative office, fiercely fought to re-establish his control over the playhouses. On June 20, 1660, he was sworn into the Mastership under Charles II and his papers give full testimony to the frantic struggles he made in an endeavour to assert his supremacy. On August 14, 1660, he came to an agreement with the Mohun group, who promised to pay him £10 immediately, £2 for every new play and £1 for every revived play, as well as £4 a week. After apparently keeping to their bargain for a few weeks, however, the actors, knowing of the pending monopoly for D'Avenant and Killigrew, decided that they no longer owed him allegiance. . . .

That gives the background to this letter which was written on 13 October to Michael Mohun at the Cockpit theatre, Drury Lane, demanding a lowering of the rates at the theatre, and the right to censor their plays. What do you think?"

"Fascinating," I conceded. "Was it actually written by this fellow Herbert?"

"Some of it at least; presumably some by his clerk, although there isn't much difference in their styles. It is the *content* which makes it such a key document in Restoration theatre history, and these manuscripts are very rare."

I still felt off-balance. "How did you arrive at the price?"

"It's provenance indicates it cost the present owner over £1,500, so with inflation and all that my advice was that £2,000 was very reasonable. She hinted she might consider a reasonable offer for a quick sale."

"You mentioned 'present owner' as though it wasn't Miss Hesse. How does she come by it?"

"Apparently she is selling it for a friend who is 'indisposed', and unwilling or unable to handle the negotiations himself. That's all she would tell me, but I can assure you it was not stolen!" He laughed with a braying sound like a donkey at the extreme unlikelihood of such a suggestion. But I had no doubt that something about it did not ring true; forewarned is forearmed.

"I'll speak to my client," I said. "If they are interested I shall come up to examine it tomorrow."

"That would be fine; I look forward to hearing from you."

In view of the strained relationship between Tom Duncan and myself, I had no intention of going to the bother of trying to track him down. In any case, *if* the manuscript was genuine I could sell it, but if I could expose it as a forgery then there could be no remaining doubt about the Lanier journal. It looked as though Charlotte had overstepped the mark through greed, or over-confidence.

Jonathon Harker produced the folio manuscript with reverence, totally unaware that I was laying a trap. I borrowed the magnifying glass and examined it closely while he looked on unsuspecting until I had finished and returned it to his desk. "Very impressive, Mr Harker, but I think that letter is a forgery."

He smiled vacuously. "You are *joking*, of course."

"On the contrary. I'm not only worried about the letter, but the circumstances in which it has been offered to me for sale — in secret and probably in

122

defiance of your company's policy."

He paled alarmingly and stammered a rebuttal. "You surely cannot believe that *I* . . ."

I shrugged. "Compared with your regular customers, I must be the least experienced in dealing with old manuscripts — yet I was singled out. Why? Because I have *one* likely customer. Some of the dealers who come here — men you're friendly with — could afford to buy it for stock, and sell it at their leisure."

"I explained that," he protested. "It was the *coincidence!*"

"Then why did our conversation have to be 'off the record'?"

"I explained that too. Strictly speaking, Chesterton's should not have been involved in a private sale."

"Especially which might be termed a 'quick' sale? Add all these features together, and it seems to have all the hallmarks of a conspiracy to defraud."

He shook his head in bewilderment. "You cannot *really* believe I would risk my reputation, and that of this company, for a measly couple of thousand pounds? Doesn't my *word* count for anything? I repeat: I was only trying to do Miss Hesse a small favour."

"You may have thought that was all it was! There is only one way to convince me — and that is by a laboratory check."

"Of course!" he exclaimed, with apparent relief. "I'm sure Miss Hesse will agree."

His anxiety reminded me that it was Charlotte I hoped to trap, not an unwitting accomplice. "I apologise, Mr Harker, if I have jumped to conclusions. I accept, of course, your assurance that you were acting in the interests of a friend, but if my

123

suspicions are confirmed, you and I will have to take some form of action."

He nodded pompously. "I could not agree more. I'm certain that Miss Hesse will be equally anxious to clear up any possible misunderstanding."

I nodded brusquely and left, walking on air.

At first sight Detective Inspector Murdoch of Ardley CID seemed a caricature of the plain-clothes country policeman; the sort depicted in an English detective novel of the 1930s. But anyone who cast him in that rôle was due for a surprise. I had good reason to respect his efficiency, and through working together we had become friends, although I had not seen him in several months. When he strolled into the shop a couple of days after my show-down with Harker, his twinkling blue eyes buried beneath shaggy blond eyebrows as he smiled in greeting, I saw him as friend, not a police officer. He was a tall, craggy individual who moved somewhat stiffly because of an arthritic condition that had set in several years ago even before his 40th birthday, but his handshake was powerful, and I always imagined him to be a strong man.

"Presumably you were bored and reckoned you could scrounge a cup of tea?" I speculated, forgetting that I had promised the police a fuller statement about the incident at Wookey Hole.

He gestured towards my sole customer. "I'm on duty, so I'm not sure I can accept your generous offer; it might be construed by some public-spirited soul as a bribe."

Realising at last why he had come, I asked him to go through to the back while I dealt with the customer — a fat little schoolboy who browsed among a handful of horror comics. "Put the kettle on. If you help yourself nobody can complain."

"On the contrary, it might look worse; extortion even," he complained. But he went through, and by the time I had got rid of my customer who had eventually read every comic for the price of one, and joined him, a pot of tea was brewing. I found some cake and biscuits. "What can I do for you?," I asked.

"Seems you are 'assisting' the police with their enquiries — for a change," he mused.

"If that is all the gratitude I get for giving you an excuse to escape from that stuffy office? I could have insisted that Wells CID came over, but I thought I'd do you a favour."

"Favour?"

"You're obviously never going to solve the phantom flasher case you've been working on for the past ten years. I thought you might like something else to take your mind off it."

"That *is* why I'm here — about the phantom flasher."

"You'll never make me confess!"

"We don't need a confession. just put your — er — *weapon* into an identiy parade. Perhaps that's why you were attacked at Wookey Hole? Trying to muscle in on another flasher's territory?" When I nodded, he added more seriously, "Seems to me, if you'll pardon a bit of detective licence, that you are *always* being attacked. In fact, that's how we met in the first place."

"Something to do with my magnetic personality; I attract people. Can't help it if some of them are villains."

He raised his eyebrows. "My advice, whatever the circumstances, is to give criminals a wide berth."

"I try. I was minding my own business and for no reason at all he attacked me!"

He finished his tea. "I saw the statement you made immediately after the attack. Must have been hair-raising."

"What do *you* think?"

He grinned, and his eyes almost disappeared again beneath the mountainous brows. "Come off it, Matt. That statement has more holes than this tea-strainer. If I had been given a single guess at the identity of the man who dictated it, I would have said 'Matthew Coll'."

"Thanks," I replied, at a loss for a more convincing reply, adding tamely, "I was in a state of shock — someone had just tried to kill me."

"So the young officer's report stated. Conscientous young man I hear, but not the most experienced. You forget I learned the hard way that you make a habit of telling the police only what *you* think they need know."

There was little point in trying to bluff him; he knew me too well. "Whatever you're implying — we didn't do so badly, you and I."

He looked exasperated. "You're at it again! 'Tell old Murdoch what a great fellow he is, and I'll have him eating out of my hand!' "

As it happened he was off the mark, but I realised I had been hoist on my own petard. I had tried to manipulate him in the past, and now it was coming home to roost. "Have they found the man who attacked me?" I asked, changing the subject.

He looked at my broken hand. "Did he do that? Or were you beating him about the head with it — to *defend* yourself, of course?"

126

I started to give him a blow by blow account of our encounter, but he stopped me. "I would rather start from the beginning. What were you doing there in the first place?"

My heart sank. I did not want to lie to Murdoch, if only because the police might by now have a record of my original telephone enquiries to Wookey Hole. I decided to play it by ear. "I was supposed to meet someone — a printer, but he didn't turn up."

"Who is this man?"

I pretended to give the matter some thought, making a show of searching through a desk-drawer for some business papers, before producing the information with a degree of mock triumph.

Having taken down Tarrant's name and address, Murdoch asked the logical follow-up question: "What was the reason for your meeting?"

I looked surprised at the question. "Business. He buys a certain amount of hand-made paper from mills like the one at Wookey Hole, and I'm interested in that quality of paper for occasional repairs to my more valuable antiquarian books. He knows the people there, and since I was going that way to do some buying it seemed a good idea to meet."

"But he didn't turn up?"

"True, but it was a loose arrangement — not as though he stood me up."

"So then what happened? Presumably you were inside."

I was relieved to leave Tarrant behind, and gave Murdoch an accurate account of what had transpired, apart from describing my assailant. After saying that I was taken by surprise, I stalled and suggested — as though it had just occurred to me —

that the Wookey Hole employee who had also been attacked may have seen him more clearly, but Murdoch shook his head. I considered taking a chance and changing my story, but Murdoch was as thorough as ever.

"Your statement says 'very tall' — *how* tall? Your height? You must be just over 6 feet?"

"*Bit* taller," I conceded. "But he was only next to me for a second, and then I was in the vat."

"He would have to be pretty strong," Murdoch speculated. "You must be about 14 stone."

"It was a question of balance."

Murdoch smiled at me mischievously. "I suppose there's no point in asking if you have any idea as to whom he might have been?"

I shook my head innocently.

"What are you doing these days — apart from running the shop?"

"Nothing much," I lied. "It's not a nine-to-five job; there's the buying to be done and the preparation of catalogues."

"All right, Matt, I'll leave it at that for the time being. If you've got problems, or there is any likelihood of another attack, for heaven's sake give me a call."

When he had gone I gave a sigh of relief. I liked Murdoch and could not afford to jeopardise our relationship, but the Lanier affair, with all its loose ends, was far too complex to explain to a policeman who dealt in hard facts, especially when I could be close to an answer.

I waited on tenter-hooks for the laboratory examination of the Herbert manuscript — and the chance to catch Charlotte Hesse 'in the act' — instead of having to wait for more elusive evidence to be uncovered. There had also been a delay in Laura's line of enquiry. When I had seen her over lunch after leaving Chesterton's, she told me that Charlotte had rung to cancel their date for the second art show. The excuse, which sounded genuine enough, had been a two-day business trip to Manchester and Liverpool. She had promised to make another date, although she had been back a few days and presumably had not telephoned.

Thinking of Charlotte Hesse reminded me of the statement I had given Murdoch. It was important that if the police contacted Tarrant, his story did not conflict with mine. I telephoned him and gave a brief account of my interview with Murdoch. It was apparent that he could not understand my attitude, and he sounded confused. I tried to reassure him. "I'm just being realistic. Apart from shielding my client from any publicity, I don't want to get involved in a prolonged hassle; it would be virtually impossible for the police to prove anything against you. As far as I'm concerned it's over and done with. We're *even*." In keeping with my pose, I did not mention the suspicion that he had murdered van der Meeren.

There was such a lengthy silence that I began to wonder if I had been talking to myself. Then when at last he spoke it was to thank me for my discretion. "If I can make it up to you in some way, I will," he insisted.

It sounded so genuine, I was tempted to claim that promise on the spot, but decided to continue the same tack, working to gain his confidence. "I told you the other day that it doesn't matter any more, although — " I tailed off as though reflecting on a nostalgic memory — "I still can't understand

129

how she expects to get away with it?"

"Who?"

"Your friend. Bet you didn't know she's come up with *another* manuscript?"

"I didn't know she had come up with *any* manuscript."

"Your loyalty is misplaced," I told him. "If you didn't know, she must have found someone else?"

But Tarrant did not react this time. He thanked me for phoning to warn him, and rang off.

I had to endure two days of waiting for news of the tests on the Herbert letter. At that point there was no longer any doubt in my mind which is why Harker's announcement came as a bombshell. "It is the genuine article, Mr Coll; I think in the circumstances . . . "

I was so stunned that I missed the rest of the sentence — something to do with sending me the invoice for the tests, since they had been carried out, without justification in his opinion, at my instigation. His tone was icy and the politeness was controlled with an effort.

I apologised, but I realised that it was not enough. I had made an enemy. I had cast aspersions on Harker's integrity, and had probably seemed unnecessarily cocky in my manner.

"I think a *written* apology to Miss Hesse is in order. You need not bother with me; dealing with ill-informed assertions and even allegations is unfortunately part of my job, but Miss Hesse is understandably upset. She has decided, as a matter of principle, that she could not now sell to you. In the circumstances there will be a change of plan, and the sale will now be handled by us in the usual way."

Tamely I apologised again, and rang off. Either Charlotte was completely innocent, in which case I did owe her a proper apology, or she had somehow pulled the rug from under my feet — and discredited me in the bargain. It meant that any accusation I made in the future about her having forged the Lanier manuscript would be dismissed as an obsession on my part. Perhaps it was?

I was so disheartened that even a call that evening from Laura failed to penetrate the thick cloud of gloom that had settled over me. She had not only met Charlotte again, but made significant progress; yet such was my mood that I found her bubbling enthusiasm faintly irritating. What did it matter now? Finally my respect for Laura and an awareness of the trouble she had taken on my behalf made me pull myself together and pay attention. It was obvious a degree of intimacy had been attained — the 'plant' I had hoped to establish in the 'enemy' camp. Perhaps the most significant information was that Charlotte had admitted she preferred the company of women, that is women of her own intellectual level. "She seemed so bitter about men," Laura reported, "I felt obliged to ask if she was gay — just so that I knew what I was getting into."

"And?"

"She's not — although she's possibly ripe for a planned seduction, even if she doesn't realise it. On the other hand there's no doubt she has had relationships with men, although on what she describes as on *her* terms — whatever that means."

I told her what had happened, and her sympathy for me was obviously tinged with relief that Charlotte had not forged the letter. "Perhaps you *are* barking up the wrong tree, darling," she suggest-

131

ed timidly, and I was conscious of the use of the word 'darling', unfamiliar in her vocabulary, to soften the criticism perhaps.

"Could be," I acknowledged. "When did you see her?"

"Last night. I got through to you at the first opportunity."

"That's interesting. Harker rang me this morning, first thing, and I gathered that he had already spoken to her. The chances are that he had the report — perhaps over the phone — yesterday. If she did know then, why wouldn't she have mentioned it to you?"

"Why should she?"

"If nothing else, as another illustration of the stupidity, aggression, I don't know, of men, or just me. In the circumstances it would have made an apt anecdote."

"More likely she didn't hear until this morning."

"Are you seeing her again?"

"I suppose so; it's down to me this time."

"Well, see if you can find out something about it — it's my last hope, and if it comes to nothing I'll have to concede defeat."

Despite her reservations, Laura agreed to have one last attempt.

Later I lay awake trying to fathom out how Charlotte had got hold of a genuine 17th-century manuscript of that rarity. I could have traced the identity of the owner through *British Auction Records* of a few years back, but without the date of the last sale, and the co-operation of Harker, which was out of the question, I would not know where to start. I thought of my friend Harry Worthington, honorary editor of the Libraries Association *Rare*

Books Newsletter. It was undoubtedly worth a call, to say that I wanted to trace a 17th-century document about the Theatre, and asking if he could give me the names of colleagues who were authorities on the subject. A librarian with that sort of expertise should know about the Herbert letter.

Worthington was as helpful as ever and had phoned me back within a half hour with information more startling than I had anticipated. The Herbert letter was not the property of any individual, but of a university library. And when he gave me the address — less than 5 miles outside Manchester — my hopes rose again. Charlotte Hesse had been to that area recently; what were the odds that the document I had examined had come from St John's? I found it difficult to concentrate on what Worthington was saying, and I pretended the line was bad so that he had to repeat certain information. " . . . told me it was bequeathed to St John's five years ago by Sir Thomas Barton, the flour tycoon you probably remember as a collector. Arthur Millard is the librarian there. In fact, Arthur and I have been on a few seminars together so please mention my name."

Frustratingly Millard was on vacation, and I had to settle for an over-cautious assistant who reluctantly gave her name as 'Miss Myers'. I ladled out the charm in huge dollops, and mentioned Harry Worthington's name as though he was Millard's closest friend, until she had relaxed sufficiently to speak off her own bat, instead of insisting that I would have to wait until Millard's return the following week. She had only been at the library for about three years and was only vaguely aware of the letter's existence. I explained that I needed to consult the manuscript urgently, and would make a special

133

trip from London for the purpose, if she was sure it was available.

Miss Myers asked me to hang on while she consulted the library index of valuable books and manuscripts, and returned apologetically to confess that the index cards were not in their file. "It is possible that Mr Millard took them out for some reason, or that they were filed in the wrong place — we do have well over 100,000 books in the building, and mix-ups can happen."

I had a feeling that the disappearance of the cards was no coincidence, but after my humiliation over the laboratory tests I decided to do nothing contentious; if necessary to err on the side of caution. "That *is* disappointing," I told Miss Myers. "I was assured that there was only one copy in existence and that was with you. Is it possible, do you think, that it is in the library, despite the breakdown of the index system?"

"It *is* possible, of course, but it means that one would have to search through hundreds of books and manuscripts in that special section. It's a question of time."

I made the right sounds. "Of course I couldn't expect *you* to look, but in view of the importance to me, could you get one of your assistants to search for it some time during the day — today if at all possible — and ring me back?"

With obvious reluctance she promised to 'see what could be done'. If the letter was missing, I realised, then almost certainly it had been stolen, and this time I would have something concrete to work on.

Later the Rev. Bill Darling popped in to tell me that the local auction-house had reacted with some enthusiasm to the books he had managed to 'restore',

134

and since Wally Crowborough, their book expert, was something of a specialist in local topography and books on hunting, it looked as though their optimism was based on reasoned judgement. "Thought you'd like to know while I was in the High Street. Got anything new while I'm here?"

I pointed to a pile of a few hundred books as yet unsorted. "Charlie Appleton managed to pick them up through a contact — contents of a private library — chap by the name of Johnson, died in Lyme Regis about a fortnight ago."

He looked at the daunting pile, and at his watch. "I think I had better display a little self-discipline and leave them for another time; I'm having my hair cut in about five minutes, so I can't really hang about."

"I don't want to lead you into temptation," I said, "but it doesn't need cutting. That *is* a waste of money."

"It's only because I'm off to London tomorrow for a conference. Don't want to be a humble vicar all my life. So my well-meaning friends tell me I should pay attention to things like my appearance — the impression I make on my Bishop and some of the VIP's they get at these functions."

I laughed. "Who *says* you don't want to be a vicar all your life?" I enquired.

"*They* do," he replied — the emphasis giving a different meaning to the answer.

"Then if you *are* serious and want to get noticed, you're going about it in the wrong way. You'll be lost in the crowd — all wearing the same outfits and the same 'short back-and-sides' haircuts. One has to be an individual to be noticed. I'd suggest a Groucho Marx moustache and cigar, and if you can walk like him, so much the better."

To my surprise he did a passable imitation. I laughed, and it suddenly occurred to me that his trip to London could be fortuitous. "How long is the conference?" I asked.

"Two days. Why?"

"Would you have time to do me a small favour?"

"I should think so — if only at lunch-times or evenings."

"This would have to be some time during the day, but it shouldn't take long." When he agreed, without even asking what it was I wanted, I had qualms momentarily about asking a clergyman to do something underhand; if not exactly lying, it certainly involved conjuring with the truth. In the event I told him the truth about the Herbert letter, about my mistaken allegation and subsequent come-uppance, and my conviction that what Charlotte had for sale had been stolen. "I would like to take another look at the manuscript but I'm not thick-skinned enough to put in an appearance just yet. Now Harker says it's going up for auction. I would be grateful if you could pose as a bibliophile — which is not in itself dishonest, and pretend you are interested in Restoration Theatre. There has been enough gossip about me over the past few days for news of its future sale to have leaked out. Go to the manuscript department — don't ask for Harker; that might be too obvious, although surely no one would suspect a vicar of being a double agent."

"Am I supposed to know precisely what the document is?"

"Good point," I replied gratefully. "That information doesn't seem to have emerged, so you'll have to be reasonably vague. But anything they tell you on or off the record, or anything you can tell from seeing it — such as distinguishing marks, stains, et cetra — would help identify it to the real owner. Would you mind that?"

"On the contrary I'm excited at the prospect. Only trouble is I'm a compulsive buyer. I might forget myself and put in a bid."

"For stolen property? I'm ashamed of you, Bill."

He consulted his watch again; obviously late for the haircut but reluctant to leave. "Ah, but if I didn't *know* it was stolen — after all, I've only got your word for it."

"Please yourself," I told him with a shrug. "Just so long as I get the information *I* want."

The Rev. Darling only left for his appointment because the phone rang to break the spell. It was Miss Myers from St John's College, reporting that she had made a search for the Herbert folio — but without success. Only Millard was in a position to decide what might have happened to it, but for the moment I was satisfied. I left a message for him to ring me on his return the following week.

EIGHT

A call from the Rev. Bill Darling the following lunch-time kept the pot boiling, but not in the way I had anticipated. His voice conveying a mixture of excitement and disappointment reported that the letter had been withdrawn.

"Why?" I was becoming conditioned to surprises.

"The only answer I could get was 'a change of heart by the owner'. Notice they did not identify him or her?"

"Intriguing," I murmured to hold his attention while I racked my brains for an explanation. "Do you know if the sale had actually been announced?"

"Funny you should ask that," he responded cheerfully. "When I arrived I made a fairly vague sort of enquiry to an assistant, but he was obviously out of his depth and referred me to your Mr Harker, who was curious about how I had heard of the manuscript. He was perfectly charming, but just a shade suspicious — enough to puncture my self-confidence, and making me feel he could see right through my act. Luckily, I had remembered what you said about impressing my 'betters' so I'd taken my Bishop with me."

"Your *what*?"

"Last night I remembered that he was a biblio-phile, so I allowed him to 'overhear' me saying I was going to Chesterton's at lunch-time — although I must admit I was speaking more loudly than usual at the time. He had never been before so he asked if he could accompany me. Very politely too."

"You cunning devil!"

"Matthew!" he protested mildly, pleased with himself.

"Sorry," I corrected myself. "You cunning old vicar."

"So even if Mr Harker did have grounds for sus-picion — and, of course, he did not — the Bishop's presence was enough to make me whiter than white."

"Did you tell him anything?"

"The Bishop? Just an outline — after all, I had to explain my own interest. Don't worry, he's on your side."

I smiled inwardly at my unlikely allies, and remind-ed him he had been in the middle of relating his discussion with Harker.

"Oh yes. Well, when he asked me how I had heard about the manuscript I mentioned the name of someone I know vaguely at Bernard Quaritch; said there had been some wild talk about a forgery."

"He accepted that?"

"Why not? If he had wanted to be discreet, he should not have been so quick to try and blacken your name; he has only himself to blame. I could not let on that I knew *which* manuscript it was, or precisely what the value was, and he made no attempt to enlighten me."

"You said something about the announcement?"

"I asked with that saintly smile of mine if he

had a catalogue, and that was when he told me the item had been withdrawn. The owner's mind had been changed — an owner's prerogative, was the expression he used — before they had been put to the trouble of putting it into a suitable auction, so that fortunately nothing had gone into print."

"The speed with which they got that manuscript off the premises sounds suspicious in itself," I pointed out. "Do you think he could be in league with her?"

"Difficult to say. I wouldn't put it past him — but then I'm biased."

"Thanks for the support, Bill, and pass on my regards to your assistant — the Bishop."

He laughed. "He's promised to come and see us — so while he is in Ardley I've no doubt we shall find our way to the shop."

"Let me know in good time," I urged. "I'll have my hair cut for the occasion."

The moment Bill had cleared the line I took a chance and rang the *Morning Herald*, asking for Charlotte Hesse. If she had answered I would have rung off, but I had a hunch she was not there, and I guessed correctly. A secretary said that she was 'out', and when I asked if I could reach her at home, as though I was a friend, she expanded enough to tell me that 'Charlotte' was out-of-town and was probably on her way back to the office now. Could she say who had called? I gave her Harker's name.

I dialled the number of St John's College Library, and when I had given my name, a worried Miss Myers came to the phone. My enquiry about the Herbert letter had upset her, especially when a senior colleague she had consulted had confirmed that the letter did belong to the library; now it was rumoured that it had gone and everyone was disclaiming responsibility. The possibility of a theft, or even loss through carelessness, discovered when the librarian was away, meant that no one knew precisely what action to take. This was the gist of the account she gave me with a degree of indignation, as though the whole mess was my fault for wanting to see it. I did my best to soothe her, pointing out that what I had to tell Millard on his return would throw some light on the matter and possibly even resolve their headache. Meanwhile, I had 'reason to believe' that another search *might* prove more successful than the last.

"I have a theory," I said, "which I cannot go into now, but which I shall explain to Mr Millard. If that theory is correct you will find the manuscript in its proper place — or if that is not easy to determine because of the confusion over your missing records — somewhere pretty near."

"But we looked once — *very* carefully. Why should it reappear?"

"I think it may have been 'borrowed' and replaced in the past day or so."

There was a short silence before the note of indignation re-emerged. "That's not possible, Mr Coll. The letter is a P classification document, which means it cannot be removed from the building!"

"I do know that, Miss Myers. But believe me: it is in the library's interests to carry out a second search. If it is not there now, then the chances are that it has been stolen, and you can imagine what a furore that will cause when Mr Millard gets back?"

This time Miss Myers offered no resistance, apparently shocked into an earnest desire to eliminate any suggestion of theft; indeed, it was evident that no book would remain unturned in the search. And it was a triumphant Miss Myers who telephoned back within a couple of hours to report that the manuscript had been found — inside the cover of a large 19th-century atlas of the world. "Goodness knows how it got in there," she exclaimed innocently, and I did not have the heart to tell her.

At last I had a few trumps in my hand, and I was determined to hold on to them until the time was right for them to be used with maximum effect. I was now convinced that Charlotte had set out to make use of the Herbert manuscript for a short period, knowing that if she could throw a spanner in the library's records system, the disappearance would probably not be noticed until someone had occasion to refer to it. The only possible incentive could be to discredit me, which in turn, since there was no material gain, would neutralise any allegation I might make in connection with the Lanier journal. None of this could be proved in a court of law, but it did at least justify my seemingly obsessional interest in her. I wondered about the extent of Harker's involvement; I could not imagine he knew about the theft, or what Charlotte was trying to do, but it was possible he had bent his company's rules to some extent to accommodate her fake story. I wondered how much she had told him, and whether she exerted any other influence over him.

The logical course was to face him across a desk, but since I was almost certainly *persona non grata*, that was easier said than done. Perhaps Wilfred Frensham could help? The next day was Saturday, but I knew him well enough to call on him at home; that would leave me free to spend the week-end with Laura. The timing, it transpired, was perfect because she was meeting Charlotte that evening, and

I could see her afterwards.

Wilfred Frensham was a man of style. As I may have said before, he looked the part, and a house in Charles Street, just off Berkeley Square is only what one would have expected. Despite his cordiality towards me, I did not know too much about his background, other than the commonly known business reputation, but had heard vaguely that he was separated, or divorced, from his wife. She now lived in the country with their three teenage children, who presumably spent term-time at the better public schools. Most of the elegant terraced houses in the road are divided into flats these days, but Frensham's lifestyle was such that he managed to occupy an entire building with just the company of a man-servant, except for when the children were visiting.

We went out to eat, although dinner was something of an anti-climax, since Frensham was to prove less co-operative than I would have hoped. I should have realised, of course, that he was very much part of the Establishment in the antiquarian book trade, ultra-conservative, and therefore disturbed at the ripples of gossip that had been set off by my un-founded allegations. In his view, the sooner the matter was forgotten the better it would be for the trade, and he saw my refusal to let the matter rest as an embarrassment. While he respected my judge-ment, and considered the evidence I presented to him 'most interesting', he was concerned that alle-gations and counter-allegations leading to ill-feeling and people taking sides would inevitably cast a shadow over the trade as a whole.

"When we first met, Matt, I remember telling you that we all have a responsibility to the trade; that to some extent we are all inter-dependent.

Any suggestions of shady dealings, let alone outright criminal activity, casts a giant shadow — makes the public *wary* of coming into shops like mine. Not so many years ago I lost a valuable customer who accused me of being involved in a well-known auction-ring. We were not; indeed, I have never resorted to that sort of buying at auction, but he had heard about the practice which was quite prevalent at the time, and assumed because of my position in the trade that I must have been one of the ringleaders.

"But surely that was different," I protested. "I know that a valuable letter was stolen for a brief period — almost certainly for the purpose of destroying my credibility. Now I am not suggesting that Harker was involved, but I want at least to draw his attention to the facts as I see them — to see how he reacts."

Frensham shook his head impatiently. "I can't stop you, Matt. But you have come to me for advice, so do at least *listen*. One: if the letter was returned, how can you ever *prove* it was missing? Two: Harker is a pompous ass, but that only makes him even more sensitive about his reputation. He has convinced himself that you are deranged, enough to tell the world — at least, his friends in the trade . . . " He broke off for a moment, and continued, "It suddenly occurred to me that if he *had* been involved it would have been in his interests to keep quiet about the incident, so he is hardly likely to approach the matter with an open mind."

"But *if* he is an honest man . . . "

"He *is* an honest man," Frensham interjected. "And I would not put it past him and Chesterton's — after all, he is a senior partner — to protect their good name by going to law if you persist."

"Good!" I retorted. "Let them sue me for defamation, or whatever, and I can produce my evidence to an impartial court."

Frensham's expression was sour. "I cannot believe you're serious."

I shrugged hopelessly. "Just bravado. I did hear what you were saying about the washing of dirty linen in public. It's just that I don't like losing."

He smiled in that paternal way of his. "I know; nor do I. That's something else we have in common. But try to look on it as a single battle, not the whole war."

"Then you're not advising me to give up?"

"You won't, whatever I say. My advice is to keep a low profile for the present. *Observe*, and be patient. If there has been some villainy down the line, they cannot have swept away *all* of the traces."

I suspected he was probably right. I would leave Harker alone and continue to concentrate on Charlotte, even though it meant relying on Laura. In any case, if Frensham reckoned it was going to be a marathon, I would have to change down a gear and take my time.

I went back to Laura's flat, using my key, and watching television until past midnight when I went to bed. I must have needed the sleep because Laura did not wake me, and when I opened my eyes at seven she was still asleep. I got up quietly and made breakfast which I took in to her on a tray. Normally Laura took fifteen minutes to get her eyes open, but for once she woke in an instant, visibly bursting with news. My carefully prepared breakfast was ignored as she sat up energetically.

"You're an inconsiderate devil," she accused, although she was so jubilant the insult managed to

145

sound like an endearment. "I rushed home to give you some really sensational news — hot off the presses — and you didn't even have the consideration to stay awake. In fact you were snoring."

"You have 'ways' of waking me up, I seem to recall."

"I didn't have the heart. You looked so exhausted, the pathetic sight brought out my motherly instincts."

"You're bringing out *my* motherly instincts," I said. "Eat your breakfast before it gets cold." To set an example, I drank my orange juice at a gulp and started on a boiled egg, and she followed suit. "What time was it?" I eventually asked.

"What time was what?"

"When you got home."

"About two."

I groaned. "I told you we country boys like to go to bed when it gets dark. I made a special concession by staying up until midnight." I finished the rest of the orange, and she stretched to kiss my mouth at the point where a trickle of juice had escaped.

"You'll never guess what *I* found out?" she demanded.

One of the shoulder-straps had dropped over her arm so that the front of her nightdress gaped forward, exposing much of her breast. "I don't feel like question-time now. I'd rather play." I looked suggestively down at her breast, and she pulled the shoulder-strap up primly.

"This is *much* more important," she retorted.

"It must be for you to turn down a proposition like that."

She ignored the crack. "What would you say if I told you that Charlotte doesn't hate men as much as she pretends? At least, not *all* men."

I pondered over the question. "If Charlotte has a lover, and you have only just discovered that fact, then she can't see him that often?"

Laura nodded encouragingly.

I thought again. "My friend Tarrant?" She shook her head, and I was prepared to give up. "The only other man I can think of is me. She must have fallen madly in love with me at the auction, as soon as she saw how dynamic I was, but she didn't want to admit it, even to herself?"

Laura finished her cup of tea and wiped her lips with a napkin before replying. "That is very possible, of course, but if so she *still* hasn't admitted it."

"Then I give up."

She pouted slightly, but then the jubilance returned. "Alexander Forbes!"

"The porn merchant — that dirty old man?"

Laura laughed. "That's not how she sees him. Nor how he sees himself."

I reflected on the unlikely match, realising that I had probably overreacted. Forbes had made his fortune by launching a couple of 'up-market' soft porn magazines that in time had become almost respectable. His interest in the sex scene had been extended to theatre, where he had successfully produced a series of typically English sex comedy shows, and he was now an impressario of international proportions, associated with 'legitimate' drama on both sides of the Atlantic, although he had never shaken off the porn image. Forbes was obviously a man of tremendous drive and business acumen, but his physical appearance was something of a let-down, being short, fat, balding and possessing the lines and skin texture of a man in his middle fifties. I pictured him from the many photo-

graphs I had seen in the media, usually with the proverbial dumb blonde showgirl towering over him, and
realised my imagination had run away with me again.
He was short, admittedly, probably no more than
5 feet 5 inches — which meant that he would not
reach beyond Charlotte's chin, but he was not fat.
That was an illusion caused by the size of his chest
and shoulders; he was in fact barrel-chested and
powerfully built. He had lost his hair early if my
memory could be trusted, long before reaching
middle-age.

"Are you listening?" Laura persisted.

"What did you find out?" I said.

"Charlotte and I had been to the cinema, and since
we went in my car we dropped off at her flat afterwards. We had coffee and brandy, and I was just
about to leave around midnight when the phone
rang. It was him — although I had no idea at the
time. All I knew was that she flushed when she spoke
to him. She said she was not alone, but added something about me being a good friend. In fact, she
didn't say much else — just listened and agreed to
something at the end, presumably a date.

"When she put the phone down she was excited,
but probably would not have said anything if I
hadn't pulled her leg about it. I don't know why they
keep the relationship a secret, whether that was her
idea or his — after all, he's not married. But she told
me, in confidence I'm ashamed to say, that they are
lovers."

"Did she say for how long?"

"I could hardly interrogate her. She wanted to
confide in someone and I happened to be around."

"Did she tell you what the attraction was?"

"That he is, for all his size, a man and a half.

Good-looking men bore Charlotte; she looks beyond appearances. But that's not all. We see *her* as being a knock-out. By Alexander's standards, in physical terms she is quite ordinary."

"I find that hard to believe."

"You're forgetting that he has always been surrounded by really beautiful women. And as a man of considerable influence to potential centre-spread models, and budding actresses, he has probably been spoiled by the richness of his diet. He told her — and it must be true because Charlotte is so wary of men — that he can't make it with dumb blondes any more. He looks for intelligence before anything else, and if there is one thing that Charlotte is constantly seeking, like your mutual heroine Emilia Lanier, it is respect."

It made sense. I was also sure that Forbes' brand of dynamism had its admirers too. So where did Tarrant fit in? I was anxious to find out. Despite Laura's insistence that it was too early to get up on a Sunday, and that she wanted to be thanked 'properly' for her news, I decided to phone Tarrant at home, before he was properly awake and on his guard.

I was lucky. The sluggishness of his tone indicated that the ringing tone had roused him from a deep sleep. I did not bother to identify myself. "I've got some interesting news about Charlotte."

I visualised him struggling to focus his thoughts. "Who is that? Oh, it's you. I was asleep. What was that about Charlotte?"

"Do you remember I told you about the other manuscript? Turns out I was wrong — it wasn't forged, it was stolen." He said nothing so I continued. "I won't bore you with the details; suffice

149

to say that it was done to discredit me. Unfortunately there's nothing I can do about it, but when I discovered she was stabbing you in the back too, the least I could do was to warn you."

"What d'you you mean?" He sounded uncertain of himself.

"Did you know she had a new lover?"

He was silent for several seconds before replying. "She's a free agent. Nothing *I* can do about it."

"That's very philosophical of you," I conceded. "I suppose we can't compete with men like him."

I pictured Tarrant struggling to contain his curiosity, before losing the uneven battle. "Let's stop playing games — who is he?" he asked irritably.

"Alexander Forbes."

I waited for his reaction, and the long silence gave him away. When he replied he tried to sound casual, but his voice was unsteady as he conceded that he had heard of Forbes. I realised he not only knew, but cared. He cared deeply.

I was banking on Tarrant being stirred to action at last, and jealously take off for Charlotte's flat for a showdown. There was the possibility he might be content with talking to her on the phone, but I knew how *I* would have reacted in that situation, and it seemed more than reasonable to suppose that he would want to be there to see her reaction. When I put the phone down I asked Laura for another favour. I did not have the car with me, and needed transport if I was going to keep surveillance outside Charlotte's flat. "It will take him a couple of hours to get dressed and down to London: I want to be there when he turns up."

"I'm not going to waste my Sunday sitting in a car all day, just to keep you company," she pro-

150

tested.

"It won't be all day," I pointed out. "He couldn't rely on her staying in, which just leaves the afternoon." I leered at her suggestively. "There's a lot of things we can do to pass the time in a car."

"In broad daylight?"

'Depends whether we're overlooked. I was about to ask you: what sort of house is it? Is there a spot we can watch without being detected?"

"It's in a square; sort of place I would like if I wasn't dependent on all the mod cons of these so-called service blocks."

"You mean if you weren't so affluent and lazy?"

Laura threw a pillow at me, but her aim was wild, and she conceded. "It is a ground floor flat in a lovely Regency house, about the size of this place, beautifully furnished . . . "

"I'm not interested in the bloody decor," I interrupted, "just the lie of the land. Now then, my little petal," (she groaned at my wheedling tone) "as a concession to your precious Sunday we'll go *after* lunch. I'll recognise his car if he has beaten us to it, and we'll wait until he comes out. They won't have too much to say to each other!"

Laura looked nervous. "The man is dangerous. I'd be happier if you stopped him."

"I think she's safe enough. My impression is that Tarrant's feelings for her are genuine — in which case he would rather suffer than see her hurt. But he will want to *know* where he stands."

My horoscope for the day must have been favourable. We had been waiting less than twenty-five minutes when Tarrant arrived and went to Charlotte's house, using his own key to get in. Laura champed at the bit while we waited for him to leave, convincing herself that her friend was being attacked by a homicidal maniac. Her anxiety was infectious, and even I was becoming restless by the time he came out again 10 minutes or so later. He drove off at top speed, convincing Laura that her fears were justified, and I agreed that before leaving the Square she could telephone Charlotte from a telephone-box in the far corner. But just as she was on the point of getting out of the car we saw Charlotte close her front door and walk down the four or five imposing steps to an MG Sprint parked outside. She got into the car, and drove off without looking left or right.

It seemed as though I had set the cat among the pigeons.

NINE

From my long observation of human behaviour patterns I would say that there are two basic types of men and women — those that *can* be classified because they fit conveniently into standard pigeon-holes, and those whose behaviour is so unpredictable they defy classification. As well as my interest in psychology you'll notice I'm also addicted to sweeping statements, and this is really another way of saying how much thought I had given to the Lanier suspects.

Strangely enough, the fact that I had discovered nothing about Charlotte Hesse did not really worry me. I did not consider her much of a problem. Charlotte was entirely consistent, and practically everything about her and her behaviour could be explained, including her attitude towards men. John Tarrant was more complex; on the face of things a Jekyll and Hyde personality, but I did not know him well enough to reach any diagnosis with confidence. I had seen two contrasting faces, both of extremes — violence and apathy. Yet as a successful businessman there had to be a third, rational and effective person. After the fearsome spectacle he had presented at Wookey Hole and St Albans, he seemed to have withdrawn into a shell, and his reaction to my goading had been sluggish to say the least. But he had been positive enough — presumably through jealousy — to call on Charlotte as soon as he heard of her association with Forbes.

Frustratingly, I could not yet pursue the tack without arousing his suspicion, if I had not already done so, but the impasse was resolved on the Tuesday. He appeared to have thrown off the lethargy when he phoned to suggest a meeting. "I'm tired of covering up for that woman," he said. "She's made fools of us both."

"Better late than never," I urged. "Where shall we meet? What about half-way, in town?"

"If you like; although if you wouldn't mind coming here, it would be more convenient because I've got to go North on business on Thursday, so it seems pointless for me to travel in the opposite direction first. Besides, I've got a few documents you missed when you searched the place."

It made no difference to me. The plaster on my left hand was beginning to feel as familiar as a glove, and it was no effort to drive the automatic, so the visit was arranged for the following evening, the Wednesday. It seemed my persistence was paying off at last.

Approaching Tarrant's home openly, through the drive and straight to the front door was an unfamiliar experience, and a reminder of something I had forgotten — the *elegance* of the house. Even so I was surprised by the slim, formal man in the white jacket who received me. Because Tarrant had been alone on the night I forced an entry it had not occurred to me that he had a servant, although from the size of the house and its well-maintained appearance it should have been obvious he needed help. The man inclined his head with deference and removed my topcoat with just the right air of polite disdain one expects of a gentleman's gentleman. With my coat neatly over one arm he led the way up a flight of stairs to a room at the first floor with imposing double doors. He opened them, waited for me to enter, and then closed them behind me. It was strange how on my previous visit — intent on looking for incriminating evidence — I had failed to appreciate the grandeur of the inside. However, despite my preoccupation with the layout and decor I was still intrigued by the servant; he had spoken only two words — "Good evening" — and yet I thought I had detected the faintest trace of a Cockney accent.

The room into which I had been ushered appeared a cross between study and library, although there was no desk as such, and the relatively few pieces of furniture were clustered around the centre in the fashion of a living-room. Tarrant rose from one of the armchairs with what might be called a 'formal' smile of welcome, thanked me for coming at short notice, and asked what I wanted to drink. This was obviously the 'third' person about whom I had speculated. He wore a faultless red velvet lounge-jacket over immaculately cut dark gaberdine slacks — the perfect example of clothes 'making' the man because they had the illusory effect of lopping six inches off his height. He seemed uncharacteristically businesslike, although when he added soda from the siphon to my whisky he was preoccupied enough to splash it over the sides of the glass. It encouraged me, yet when he handed me the drink I noticed his

155

hand was perfectly steady.

I suppose I was too interested in the room to dwell on the apparent change in the Tarrant image. It was quite huge, at least 30 feet by 20 feet, with a floor-to-ceiling veranda window opening on to a balcony at the front. Heavy ruby velvet drape curtains were drawn, imparting a warmth to what might otherwise (because of its size) be a chilly room, and this was accentuated by the row upon row of leather-bound books, some behind glass, others immediately accessible on open shelves, although I knew this was only the tip of the iceberg representing his collection. While the room was sparsely furnished, everything in it — armchairs, rugs, occasional tables, standard lamps — seemed massive, making the space less daunting and the overall impression one of comfort.

I complimented him on his home, but it seemed he barely heard, and I suspected he was more affected by the news of Charlotte's new relationship than he had admitted. From the constant flexing of the muscles in his jaw and the stiffness of his shoulders, it was evident he was under strain, and not for the first time I reflected on the power women can have on some men. I sipped my whisky in silence until it was obvious he was making no effort to get to the point, and I slipped in a gentle reminder. "You wanted to tell me something about Charlotte."

He stared at me glassily. "Funny how otherwise intelligent people can have such difficulty controlling their biological urges — something the average yobbo loses no sleep over. I'm not inexperienced with women, yet whenever I drop my guard I seem to get punished for it. My wife was a prize bitch."

I was not particularly interested in the former Mrs Tarrant. The drive from Ardley had been tiring, and the comfort of the armchair and the generous measure of whisky was more conducive to a relaxing evening alone with my thoughts or listening to music than being obliged to contend with Tarrant crying on my shoulder. Yet now that he was prepared to talk at last I dared not interrupt. I turned a deaf ear to some of his maudlin reminiscences, and waited impatiently for him to get round to Charlotte. Even then he made a meal of it, boring me with an interminable account of the way they had met at an auction, what she was wearing, what they had said to each other, and how the relationship had developed. It was an effort to restrain myself from telling him to get a move on, or to hint at it with an ostentatious yawn; in fact I had to stop myself from yawning in any way at all.

I must have been on the verge of blatant rudeness when he stopped talking and lapsed into silence, staring dejectedly at the floor for several seconds before rising and pouring himself another drink. The sudden action recaptured my attention, and while he seemed wrapped up in himself I studied his back. The shoulders were slumped in a way that did not suggest tiredness alone. But then he seemed to pull himself together and returned with a refill for me, although he had not asked if I wanted another drink. He continued to stand, leaning against the high back of an armchair, and stared down at me for a few seconds before continuing: "I admire you, Matt — you didn't get involved with her. It's safer that way."

I nodded to humour him, and interjected a question more to the point. "Whose idea was it to forge the Lanier journal?"

He shook his head miserably. "I was just a pawn.

We're *all* pawns in this business."

Suddenly I was very tired and confused. *Who* were all pawns? I was overwhelmed by a sense of frustration. Emilia Lanier had dominated my thoughts in recent weeks, yet I seeemed to be on a treadmill getting nowhere. I was really very tired, weary of the whole business. My mind rebelled at having to contend with constant suspicion and aggravation, pushing on to the side-lines the ideas for which I had left London. I told him very firmly how I felt. "I've just wasted a whole slice of my life. It's time to cut my losses. Either I find out whatever there is to know *now* — this week, this *minute* — or I give up, forget I ever heard of Emilia Lanier."

He nodded stonily. "Good idea."

I was intensely irritated by his complacency. "But I can't make that decision until I've got answers to certain questions," I pointed out. "Just be a good chap and answer — yes or no."

Tarrant seemed so difficult to pin down; he was sitting there politely a few feet away, but I knew I had to spell it out to him very simply so there could be no misunderstanding. I concentrated hard and spoke very deliberately as though he were a child.

"Question one: is the Lanier jounal genuine, or is it a forgery? Come on now, Tarrant — yes or no?"

"Yes or no *what*?"

I felt as though I was drowning in jelly. "Is it a forgery?"

"Yes."

I sighed as though a tremendous weight had been lifted from my shoulders. At last I was getting somewhere. I concentrated again. "Now you can see how much easier it is when you just answer 'yes' or 'no'? Question two: You said you were just the pawn,

158

but did you provide the *paper*?"

He nodded.

"And the ageing, binding, et cetera et cetera?" The way I spelled out the words, slowly and with deliberation seemed appropriate to the occasion, as though they carried the due weight and solemnity of the law. I wondered whether I was overdoing the theatricals — surely it was not necessary to slur my words? Perhaps I'd had too much to drink? Two doubles? Never.

I concentrated again. "And it was Charlotte who put pen to paper — did the actual *forging*, if you know what I mean" I could not be bothered to complete the sentence — he would know what I meant.

But he seemed to have forgotten his promise to answer only 'yes' or 'no'. "How do I know you won't go to the police? I need a promise that my part in the affair can be swept under the carpet?" At least I think that was what he said; something else about Queen's evidence. Frankly I did not want to think about Tarrant's problem; I had problems of my own, and I didn't want to think even about them now. What must have been a delayed reaction to the events of the past weeks was creeping up on me fast, and I felt more than tired — I felt ill. If I didn't get some fresh air quickly I'd embarrass myself by falling asleep in the armchair. Even as the picture flashed through my mind, it became an effort to keep my eyes open. I stood up quickly — too quickly, it seemed, and was suddenly dizzy. I sat down again, mumbling an apology, and had to lie back for a moment.

When I opened my eyes, the weights seemed to have

159

been lifted, although I had a shocking headache and a foul taste in the mouth. I felt an idiot at having dozed off in front of Tarrant, and wondered how he had reacted. I tried to sneak a surreptitious look, but when my head would not turn in his direction I discovered I was no longer in the chair — I was lying on the floor, face down. In pulling myself on to my knees I became aware of a heavy brass paper-weight in the shape of a Celtic cross clutched in my hand. It was bloodstained.

I dropped it instinctively and looked about me. Only two or three feet away Tarrant was lying on his back, his face horribly battered. I could see from the fixed expression that he was dead. I was stunned, and my mind seemed to react in slow motion. Should I call an ambulance? No, I realised that was not a priority; I didn't have to examine him to know that he was beyond help. But then if someone had killed him the police had to be informed without another second's delay. They would want to set up roadblocks, or something. No, roadblocks did not come into it. Airports perhaps. I got to my feet unsteadily and looked around for the phone. Two of the armchairs and other pieces of furniture had been turned over in what must have been a terrible struggle. I tried to picture what might have happened, but the effort was diverted by spotting the phone in the corner.

I moved in that direction and stumbled over something which turned out to be the paper-weight. The murder weapon! My head suddenly cleared. The cross had been in my hand when I recovered consciousness. I panicked for a split second. They would obviously think it was me. I *knew* I hadn't attacked Tarrant, even in the midst of a black-out.

160

Ominously it began to look as though I had been framed. Who would believe I had dozed off? What d'you mean, *dozed* off? I had been drugged! Tarrant for some reason had slipped something into my drink.

I looked round for the whisky and the glasses, which would at least confirm my story, but there was no sign of them. The hairs on the back of my head began to stand up. I had been led into a trap. Goodness knows how long I had been unconscious. The police were probably on their way at this moment. I had to get out immediately. But on reaching the door I remembered I had a coat somewhere in the house. Where was that bloody manservant? More to the point, why hadn't he heard the sounds of the struggle upstairs? Perhaps he was dead too, or perhaps he had been involved? I visualised the man carefully setting the scene, putting the paper-weight in my hand. I had to do something about those finger-prints.

At that moment the front doorbell rang. It had to be the police. Did I run — or cover my tracks first? I decided to go, calculating that my finger-prints would not mean anything if the police had nothing with which to compare them. The front of the house was out of the question, so I would have to find a window or door at the back, or perhaps an exit to the printing-works. The police were now hammering at the front door, and it was obvious that Tarrant's manservant was not around to deal with the racket — or able to do so. In another few minutes they would probably give up being correct and force an entry.

I hurried out of the room on to the landing where I could see the silhouettes of men on the pavement through the glass panel above the wooden street-door. One of them looked up. Could he see me? The landing light was on. I daren't wait any longer. A hasty glance down at the coat-stand in the lobby below revealed no sign of my coat, so I made for the back. The first door led to a bedroom where I found a window overlooking a tiny walled-off section of the garden. It was perfectly quiet below, and a drain-pipe immediately outside the window, set into the brickwork with brackets that seemed quite secure, seemed to offer the ideal escape route. I climbed from the sill on to the pipe and then clambered down to the ground quite easily. Too easily, of course. Out of the shadows on either side of me stepped a policeman. Each grabbed an arm firmly, and even as I contemplated trying to break free another pair of plain-clothesmen arrived.

I was dragged unceremoniously round to the front of the house, and in through the door which had been forced. It happened so quickly that not a word was exchanged. I did think of protesting my innocence, but the words that occurred to me sounded ludicrous, and I realised no one would believe me. In the hallway, one of my captors, a mean-looking character who had me by the collar, called out: "We've got him, Sir."

Men seemed to spill curiously from several rooms, but a disembodied voice from the drawing-room upstairs instructed him to bring me up. We found "Sir" squatting on his haunches over the body of Tarrant. He did not seem terribly distressed by the injuries, and looked up casually as we entered. Then, somewhat stiffly he got to his feet, rubbing his back with a grimace. He was a tall, rather good-looking man with a ruddy complexion, probably in his late forties: the sort of man who might once have been very fit but now no longer bothered to 'work off' a hefty consumption of alcohol. He regarded me soberly. "I'm Inspector Palmer. Who are you?"

I gave him my name.

He gestured with his head at the body. "Do you know who this is — was?"

I answered him, explaining that we were in the dead man's home.

"What can you tell us about it?" He waved his hand expanisvely to take in the room. " — That is, what happened to Mr Tarrant?"

I shrugged. "Not much. I found him like that. It obviously came as a shock, and I must have been standing here like an idiot for some time. Then you arrived. I realised what your reaction must be — and I panicked. It was foolish of me, but I knew my story was going to be pretty hard to swallow."

The Inspector rubbed his back irritably, and squatted by the body again. He lifted Tarrant's hands one by one and examined the fingertips carefully before rising. He pressed both knuckles against his spine, and said by way of explanation, "Damned back. Doctors don't know the first thing about them. Tell you to lie on a hard board. I ask you . . . " He looked at me questioningly, but without really wanting an answer, so I waited expectantly. "Been in a fight?" he added indifferently.

I nodded. "I was attacked recently — at a paper-mill in the West Country. The local police know all about it."

"I'm sure they do, Sir," he answered sympathetically, "but those scratches could not have been made then. They haven't even been cleaned up yet."

His stare was directed at my face, and I put my hand up instinctively. My fingers found thick lines of what appeared to be congealed blood, and I traced them for several inches.

He smiled. "What odds would you give that the skin and blood under Mr er — whatever his name is — under the deceased's fingernails matches the marks on your face?"

The evidence was now too overwhelming for it not to be anything other than a frame unless I could be provided with a strong motive, and I said so. "I know it is an overworked plea, but this time it's true. Quite apart from the police at Wells, practically everything in my story can be confirmed by Inspector Murdoch at Ardley, who knows me personally. I happen to be very much on the side of law and order, and I have no possible reason for killing Mr Tarrant." I gave him an edited report of my 'investigation' to date. To his credit he listened patiently and appeared to accept it on its face value.

"I'll speak to Murdoch," he conceded, "but meanwhile the facts are inescapable. You were caught running away from the scene of a murder, with bits of your skin — let's just make that assumption for the moment — under the fingernails of the deceased. It would have to be a pretty elaborate frame?"

I nodded.

"So in the circumstances I'd be obliged if you will come down to the station while we continue our enquiries. Do you want to call a solicitor?"

I shrugged. "Inspector Murdoch is the key. I'll decide when you've spoken to him."

At the City police station I was taken to a bare interview-room with the customary wooden table and two chairs and left alone with a cup of tea. I spent the time trying to compose the statement they would inevitably want. The 'whole' truth seemed so implausible, but to embellish it might lead to further complications. The problem had still not been resolved when Palmer returned.

"'Fraid we're going to have to ask you to stay the night," he announced breezily. "We'll fix you up with a proper bed and something to eat."

I was stunned. "But what about Inspector Murdoch. Have you spoken to him yet?"

He nodded. "He confirmed some of your story, but he couldn't comment on your relationship with Tarrant. More to the point, we've since found some new evidence."

"That impossible!"

He ignored the interruption. "Who is Charlotte?"

"Charlotte Hesse?"

He shrugged. "I'm asking *you*?"

"I don't get the connection, but if it's Charlotte Hesse you mean, then she's someone I know — vaguely. She is a journalist on one of the national dailies."

"How vaguely?"

I responded irritably. "She interviewed me once. What has she got to do with this?"

Again he seemed to ignore my protest. "And did she also know Mr Tarrant vaguely, or more than vaguely?"

"They may have been lovers. If it's important, then ask the lady."

"We will, but independent corroboration never hurts. What was *your* attitude to their relationship?"

"Total indifference."

"Is she an attractive young lady?"

165

"If you're hinting that I killed him in a jealous rage, you'd better think again."

"Stranger things have happened, Mr Coll. And, after all, you did threaten him."

"Rubbish."

"Come now, Mr Coll. We have the letters."

I was stunned. "What are you talking about?"

He shook his head sadly at my apparent lack of co-operation, suddenly grimaced and remembered to rub his back. "I'm waiting for photostats."

I groaned. "Next thing you'll come up with is a receipt demonstrating that I bought the murder weapon — the paper-weight — if that's what it was — or the knife, or the gun, or the bloody poison that killed him."

"So you're sticking to your story about being framed?" he enquired politely.

I sighed. "Where are these letters supposed to have been found. Under the body?"

A flicker of annoyance crossed his face. "We're just doing a job, Mr Coll. If you must know, we searched the man's papers and found them in different places."

"Very diligent of you," I said bitterly. I looked at my wrist-watch. It was past midnight. God, what was happening? "You haven't told me yet, Inspector, how you came to arrive on the scene of the crime so conveniently — practically in time to catch me red-handed."

"A 999 call reporting sounds of an argument and fight — someone walking past the house."

"We must have been fifty yards from the road."

"Sound carries at night."

"Anonymous caller, of course?"

"Doesn't make it any less valid. We get them all

166

the time; people who just don't want to get involved."

"But even if you got here in a couple of minutes, I *should* have had time to clear up and get away."

"What is that supposed to mean?"

"That I was drugged. And while I was out they had the opportunity to stage anything they wanted — right down to dialling 999 at just the right moment. Wouldn't have done for you to have found me asleep."

He shrugged, opened the door and shouted. Almost at once a detective came in clutching a note-book. "It's time we took a statement," announced Palmer, "then we can see what's what."

There was a sinking feeling in the pit of my stomach, but in that moment I decided to keep to the facts — they were too bizarre to have been invented. I started with the phone call, finishing with my abortive escape attempt. As an afterthought I listed my various suspicions, concluding on a question. "Why would I have bothered to even *mention* things like the drugged drink — when it's so obvious the glasses have disappeared, or been cleaned?"

Palmer's expression was difficult to determine. "Sometimes the crazier a story seems, the easier it is to swallow — for obvious reasons."

The tough-looking detective who had apprehended me came in and handed some sheets of paper to Palmer, whispered in his ear and then took up a position just behind me. I was conscious of him staring at my neck, and had a disconcerting feeling that he might suddenly grab me. The Inspector studied the papers for a moment and then seemed to remember something. "We'll have to wait for the constable to get that statement typed, but first let me clarify one point. Did you say something about being admitted by Tarrant's manservant — the man who took your coat?" I nodded, and he continued, "The gentleman in question apparently just got home. It seems he was given the evening off, so obviously he doesn't remember seeing you."

My spirits lifted. "That simply proves the man I saw was an impostor."

Palmer shook his head. "Or that you made the whole thing up." He produced the sheets of paper, kept two and handed me photostats. The first thing I noticed was that the short letters had been typed on my headed paper. The top one, dated two weeks earlier, read:

Dear Tarrant,

Since you're never 'available' when I phone these days I've got to put something on record. This is intended as one last appeal to leave Charlotte alone. She is finished with you for good, so don't try to mix it. While we can't claim to be friends, I thought we at least respected each other. So let me appeal to that respect. *Please* leave her alone. I don't want to demonstrate the unpleasant side to my nature."

The second letter, dated only a few days ago, continued in the same vain:

'. . . I tried to be civilised over Charlotte, but you're even more of a shit than I realised, so it looks as though I'll have to fight fire with fire. If I don't get an undertaking by return you'll wish we'd never met.'

Both were signed M. Coll in a passable imitation of

168

the way my surname is written, except that I always prefix it with 'Matt' or 'Matthew', depending on whom I address. I got the impression that the idiosyncrasies of my full signature had proved too much of a headache — presumably through inadequate preparation. In fact, the whole job looked uncharacteristically unprofessional, as though it might only have been done as an afterthought, an additional flourish. The letterhead was undoubtedly mine, but it was clear the letters had not been typed on my machine. I told him so.

Palmer gave the photostats back to the detective who had brought them, and instructed him to have them despatched urgently to Inspector Murdoch. He said something about telephotos to regional headquarters, and then messenger to Ardley. It was the first thing he had said that was reassuring. When he had gone, Palmer turned to me. "Why would they bother to use your notepaper and slip up on the typewriter?"

I shrugged. "It's not difficult to pinch a few sheets of notepaper. It takes longer to compose and type letters."

I could see that despite his impassivity, he was inclined to believe my story, because he began to show signs of embarrassment. "*If* Ardley police confirm the typefaces don't match up, I've got to take a decision — whether to charge you on the evidence we've got, which is, admittedly, circumstantial — or let you go for the time being while we continue our enquiries. Either way, I must ask you to stay until the morning."

"*Ask* me? You mean I have a choice?"

He smiled. "Should we decide to charge you, I've still got to check out one or two points which will take another couple of hours. There's a limit to how long we can hold someone without pressing charges."

I didn't really have much option. I could stand on my dignity, and demand my 'rights'. What for? The privilege of walking out into the chill of the early hours — to face a two-and-half hour drive home? Goodness knows where my topcoat was, and I could only hope the car was still parked in Tarrant's drive.

I did not consider I had the right to ring Laura at this hour, and the thought of a run-of-the mill hotel was little more reassuring than the accommodation being offered to me now — with the compliments of the police. Palmer looked relieved that I was prepared to be 'reasonable'. He was also going off duty and said that he would see me in the morning.

At seven I was awakened with tea and toast. The bed had been small but comfortable, and I had slept reasonably well. I was allowed to freshen up, but then had to kick my heels with just a morning newspaper until Inspector Palmer put in an appearance just before 10 a.m. There was nothing in the paper about Tarrant's death, and one of the constables told me that the news had not been released. Palmer sauntered in, shaking his head wearily and rubbing his back. "Morning," he announced, his voice hoarse. "Sorry to have kept you hanging about. You're free to go for the moment. Condition is that we know where to find you at any time. If you go home, you'll need to keep in touch with Ardley CID."

His indifference annoyed me. "What I do from now on," I replied indignantly, "depends on you. One minute you talk about charging me with murder,

170

the next tell me to go without a word of explanation. I can't blame you for being suspicious in the first place, but I'm entitled to know what changed your attitude."

Palmer was unrepentant. "All I know is that we've got a dead man on ice, and we've got to find his killer. You're still the prime suspect — in the absence of anyone more suitable. I happen to believe your story — partly because of what Inspector Murdoch said, but there are a thousand-and-one loose ends. Your fingerprints on the paper-weight, your coat in a cupboard indicating that you didn't just walk in and fall over the body . . ."

"Where is my coat, by the way?" I interrupted.

"You can collect it from forensic on the way out."

"Presumably you couldn't match those letters with my typewriter?" When he shook his head, I wondered irrelevantly how the police had got in , but it didn't seem worth prolonging the discussion. Instead I told him that I had to get back to Ardley, but would do as he requested and stay in touch with Murdoch.

He studied me for a second or two as though trying to reach a decision, and then picked up the phone, asking to be connected to Ardley Police. He gave Murdoch what I thought was a reasonably fair account of the developments, and added that I was being allowed to go, on condition that I kept in contact with him. Eventually he passed the phone over to me, and Murdoch asked what my plans were. Relieved to be talking to a familiar, and friendlier voice, I felt a lot better. I told him the truth — that I was going back to the shop for a bath and shave. "You can get me there if I'm needed," I told him.

171

TEN

So much had happened within such a short space of time that I was disconcerted by the apparent normality of life outside the police station. The sun was shining, signalling the start to a fine day, and people hurrying to work brushed past me without a glance. It was hard to accept that nobody knew or cared about what I had been through. It was like a bad dream, and I just wanted to go home and lick my wounds. Then the alternative attraction of a bath and shave at Laura's flat before the long drive back asserted itself. The delay of a few hours at most would surely not worry Murdoch, if indeed he was ever to know.

Laura was at work by the time I got to the flat and I let myself in. I phoned her at the office, told her what had happened, and had difficulty in preventing her from coming back to be with me. I would have welcomed her warmth and love, but I was physically unharmed and did not want to take advantage of her thoughtfulness. "You know what this means?" I asked after completing my account of Tarrant's death, and supplying my own answer: "A couple of days after a showdown with

Charlotte, Tarrant is killed. There has to be a connection."

"Charlotte was with me last night," Laura replied.

I almost surrendered to a fit of depression at the way everything seemed to work in Charlotte's favour; now even my closest friend was unwittingly supplying her with an alibi. Then common sense prevailed; I realised that Tarrant's death had been arranged by professionals. I had seen at least one of them, the man who had posed as his butler. The butler is always the murderer, I thought.

Nevertheless, I decided that after the bath and a rest I would pay Charlotte a visit. It was time to take the action to the very heart of 'enemy' territory. I phoned her office a couple of times during the afternoon, and when I was confident she had left for home, drove to the Square and waited for her to return. I gave her five minutes' grace and rang the front-door bell.

She was surprised to see me. "Mr Coll . . ."

"Matt," I corrected. "After all we've been through together I think we ought at least to be on Christian name terms."

Her look of amazement was genuine. "I'm sorry."

"May I come in?"

She stood aside from the door and allowed me to pass. "Straight through to the left," she instructed. The drawing-room was what I had expected from Laura's description — if anything underfurnished; but each object had been chosen with care. It was like a setting from Ideal Home and I guessed that some of the designs represented top names in the business. It was all very swish, although my admiration was muted by an uncomfortable feeling that I should have wiped my shoes more carefully on the mat outside.

She gestured to an armchair and asked if I would like some form of 'refreshment'. Her manner was so courteous I might have believed she regarded me as just another casual caller, or a book-dealer she had interviewed at an auction some weeks before and to whom she had not given another thought.

I declined the offer and apologised for calling uninvited. "I felt we knew each other so well by now that I could dispense with formalities."

The puzzled expression returned. "Mr Coll — Matt. Didn't we meet just the once?" I nodded and her remarkably pale blue eyes widened. "And I gave you my address?"

I smiled. "My ego would like to say that you insisted on giving me your phone number and address, but since I hope we're going to be truthful I'll admit I followed Tarrant here on Sunday."

As the curiosity in her face was replaced by an expression of guarded neutrality, I remembered she would not yet have heard of his death. I could not have wished for a better opportunity to catch her off guard, but decided to keep the news as an ace up my sleeve.

"What do you want?" Her tone gave nothing away.

"Answers, for a start. I suppose a confession would be too much to ask."

She stood up. "I think you had better leave, Mr Coll. I find your supercillious manner, especially the innuendo that we know each other in some special way, offensive."

She was so self-confident that I could see I was unlikely to penetrate those carefully erected defences by a frontal attack. Probes cloaked in charm would be picked off from a distance, but I suspected

174

there might be another way. I apologised for the unfortunate start to our discussion. "I'm afraid I'm rather hide-bound in my attitude to the weaker sex. Normally I call a spade a spade, but wrongly as it turned out I decided to handle you with kid gloves. I don't like to think of women as criminals." I could see she found my chauvinism irritating, but to her credit managed to control the angry retort on her lips. I pressed on, using the same weapon. "I don't know why a beautiful woman like you had to get mixed up in this nasty business. You're obviously intelligent." I nearly added 'for a woman', but decided that the hint of patronage might be more convincing than outright rudeness. It worked because she felt obliged to say something to relieve the strain of keeping her temper in check.

She tried sarcasm. "You flatter me!"

I pretended to be surprised at her attitude. "I'm sorry if that sounded patronising." And to rub it in I added, "I think women can be every bit as intelligent as men — sometimes even more so." It had much the same effect as a fascist telling a Jew that 'some of my best friends are . . .'

If looks could have killed I would have dropped dead on the spot. "What is this leading up to, Mr Coll — a proposal of marriage?"

I smiled ruefully. "I'm sure you have your sights higher than me. With your looks, *and* brains, you could marry anyone. That's why I can't believe you did it for the money. If money was the goal, there are men — rich men."

"You see me as a kept woman?"

"Wife."

"Same difference."

I pretended not to notice the contempt in her

voice, taking her answer on its face value. "I gather you're the independent sort? Very commendable. I admire women who don't conform to the rôle society imposes on them." I flinched inwardly at the sunny good nature of my tone as though I had turned back the clock seventy-five years and was trying to humour a suffragette. "But that cannot excuse breaking the law. Surely you can see that?"

I was conscious of her taking a deep breath as she tried to pull herself together. "Are you *trying* to be unpleasant? Or is this the way you normally behave?" She stood up, a signal for me to leave.

I shrugged, remaining where I was. "I'll come to the point. I believe you helped Tarrant forge the Lanier manuscript that cost my clients £68,000."

She did not turn a hair. "If that is what you believe, then nothing I can say will alter that belief. I suggest you go to the police."

"I have — or rather they came to me. There has already been what politicians describe as a 'full and frank' exchange of views. They are more interested at the moment in Tarrant, and I didn't tell them about you because I believe that you were exploited. Goodness knows what web of lies he spun to ensnare you: or were you just infatuated?"

The frayed strands of her temper finally snapped and her right hand snaked out to slap me. I was prepared and raised a forearm to block it. Her momentum and my swaying movement inside brought us together, and suddenly the pent-up anger transformed her from a beautiful but depressingly earnest young woman into an animated bundle of energy that pulsated with sexual magnetism. On impulse I kissed her. Beneath the raging fury I detected in her an undercurrent of excitement, and sensed that if the

176

struggle continued it might have ended in rape — to the humiliation of us both. Fortunately her flailing fists gave me something to think about, no small problem with only one effective hand, but I was finally able to pin both wrists behind her back. Although she continued to struggle I was too strong for her.

"You bastard!" she spat.

"I'm not going to touch you — you're quite safe."

"For how long?"

I relaxed the pressure on her wrists slightly. "I'll cut out the insults if you calm down. Just answer my questions."

"Your *questions* are insulting."

"I asked if you were Tarrant's partner — you only had to answer yes or no."

She seemed to relax imperceptibly. "John Tarrant was my lover — yes. The answer to the other part of your question is 'no'. If he had anything to do with forging that manuscript *I* never knew."

"But the forgery was the work of a woman. If it wasn't you, then who was it?" I let go of her wrists uneasily.

She rubbed them briskly, but when she looked up at me again anger had been replaced by the old composure. "You seem to have an obsession about forged manuscripts," she said.

"Hardly surprising in the circumstances."

"What you believe doesn't really bother me, although it might explain your strange behaviour. The fact is that I knew nothing about your forgery, and I don't see why I should have to deny it."

"Forget that for a moment. What about the manuscript you took to Jonathon Harker? Wasn't that whole incident stage-managed for my benefit — embarrassment, if you prefer?"

"You must have a persecution complex. I had a letter for sale and took it to Jonathon. He suggested I might save time and money by offering it to you. We didn't reckon on your obsession."

I admired her composure. "I walked right into it, bloody fool."

She looked exasperated. "Into what?"

"If I was such a logical customer why didn't you come straight to me instead of going through a third party?"

"It did occur to us . . . "

"Us?"

"The owner is a collector; he knew about the Lanier sale and suggested your American university might be interested. On reflection he thought we should capitalise on Jonathon's advice."

"Had Harker been in touch with you before that? Did he tell you, for example, that I had been making enquiries about you?"

"Of course. He couldn't wait to tell me. You should know what an old woman he is."

"And was this mentioned to your collector friend by any chance?"

"It may have been. What has that got to do with it?"

It was my turn to be annoyed at her persistence in denying the obvious. "Come off it, Charlotte. A few moments ago I set out to provoke you. I hoped you would lose your temper and admit complicity because you were *proud* of what you'd done, more than ashamed. I apologised. But now I'm putting all my cards on the table. I'm obviously not going to get a confession, but don't insult my intelligence by denying you stole the Herbert manuscript. It's over and done with, so there's nothing I can do about it."

She seemed bewildered and I was reasonably sure it was not an act. "What I told Jonathon was true. I was selling it on behalf of a friend."

"And you didn't know it was stolen?"

"What on earth gave you that idea?"

"Because there is only one copy in existence, and that belongs to St John's College library — which you well know. Yours had to be a forgery or the original — which did not belong to a private collector."

For the first time she began to look unsure of herself. "I can't answer that."

I laughed. "Of course not. As soon as I learned, the hard way, that the letter was genuine I rang St John's, and guess what? The letter was missing. And guess who happened to have been in Manchester at that time? *And* who happened to be out of town when it was returned?"

"If you mean me, you ought to know that I have to go to the provinces several times a month. I did go to Manchester, to an exhibition, but on the second occasion I was nowhere near; in fact I was in Stoke. I can produce a number of witnesses from both places."

"Just a coincidence," I said with heavy irony.

"Evidently. I can see now why you jumped to conclusions, but I've told you the truth."

I looked at her hopelessly. She was either a brilliant actress or telling the truth. "You win," I conceded. "Short of taking you up there and parading you in front of the library staff, there is no way I can prove you stole the letter — yet stolen it was."

The genuine frustration in my voice must have been more effective than my interrogation. Her attitude softened. "If it makes you any happier, I'll come with you if it can be arranged to coincide with my next visit North. I've nothing to hide; I've never been to St John's college in my life."

The offer floored me. Momentarily I thought of her in dark wig and glasses, but she appeared to read my thoughts. "I've never been there — even in disguise. It seems that from the start you have made assumptions about me, and then searched for so-called evidence that would substantiate those assumptions."

I was beginning to feel uncomfortable; there was more than an element of truth in what she said. "But if you had nothing to do with the Lanier journal," I asked, half-heartedly, "who did?"

She shrugged. "How should I know? I came to the sale because I was fascinated by Emilia Lanier, and even did some research — but it never occurred to me that the manuscript might have been forged until you mentioned it. What evidence is there?"

"You didn't know that Tarrant tried to kill me?"

"Good God! Of course I didn't know."

I told her the whole story, and how my suspicions had first been raised by the murder of van der Meeran. I concluded with the news I now had less assurance in relaying — Tarrant's murder.

The news shocked her, although it was obvious that any feelings she may once have had for Tarrant had changed. After the initial shock she managed to mask whatever emotions might have been experienced. "What happened?" she enquired.

I told her. "I was so convinced you were partners my initial reaction was that you might have killed him."

"Why on earth should I want to do that?"

180

"After what you've told me today, the theory no longer stands up. It seems likely that Tarrant killed van der Meeren, and if you two weren't partners-in-crime then I'm back to square one."

"Are you even sure that van der Meeran's murder was connected with the Lanier journal? I don't know what the statistics are for murders in Holland, but they must be high enough to support the possibility of coincidence — especially after what you've just learned about coincidences."

I sighed. "The Dutch police think there's a connection, and they have no axe to grind."

"I'm sure they know what they are doing, but why pick on Tarrant and me?"

"Because there *is* no one else apart from me, and I wouldn't go to these lengths to lay a trail of red herrings. Besides, Tarrant admitted his part before he was killed — which left just you. And although I now accept that you didn't steal the Herbert letter, we have not yet resolved how it came to appear on the scene at just that moment, and was withdrawn as soon as I had been made to look a fool." I stopped as it occurred to me I was missing a significant piece of information. "I was so preoccupied with your involvement I forgot about the letter," I told her. "There is only one, and that belongs to the College library — which means that *someone* stole it before giving it to you to sell. I'd like to speak to the person who claims to be the owner."

She shook her head. "I'm sure there is an explanation, and I intend to find out. Meanwhile, I will not betray a trust."

"But it was stolen," I protested.

She smiled. "You've made a number of sweeping allegations, mainly against me. Don't you think you *owe* me the benefit of the doubt in this one issue? I'll let you know the explanation."

It was evident I would not budge her, so I took the question as my cue to leave. I had never dreamed I would have to resort to placing my trust in Charlotte Hesse.

As I came down the steps into the Square, my heart sank at the approach of two men who had been waiting in a parked dark green Rover 3500. About my own age, one was dressed in a dark blue blazer and grey slacks, and the other in a three-piece brown pin-stripe suit. I thought they had the look of plain-clothes police about them, and could imagine Inspector Palmer's triumph at catching me out so quickly in a visit to a material witness I claimed to know only vaguely — not to mention Murdoch's anger at my broken promise to return to Ardley. I could imagine his pained expression. "You didn't have to *lie* to me."

The man in the blue blazer stepped into my path. "Excuse me, sir. Would you be Mr Matthew Coll?"

I nodded. "I was on my way back to Ardley now — just made a slight detour through London."

I cursed myself for being so apologetic, not even knowing what they wanted, but they did not comment and the spokesman asked if I would 'mind' accompanying them. It was, of course, phrased in a way that gave me no option, but they were just doing a job, not trying to be difficult, because when I pointed to my car parked about fifteen yards away they conferred and decided I could follow, with the man in brown as my escort. In the car he looked down pointedly at my hand in plaster as though

182

making a mental note to add yet another crime to the long list prepared in my absence, but he said nothing. In fact, he was an uncommunicative devil, choosing not to respond to my polite conversation, even when I asked very politely to which police station we were headed.

In particularly heavy traffic, it had taken us twenty minutes before we turned into the outer perimeter road of Regent's Park. Instead of speeding up, the Rover in front slowed and pulled into the kerb by a group of terraced houses. I followed his lead, stopped and was ushered out by my escort. I followed them to the first house in the row, a delightful cream building with huge picture-bay windows, set behind a fenced-in paved garden. This was no police station, and I realised with mounting irritation that I had again jumped to conclusions. Because I had expected the CID to call at Charlotte's house, I had not even asked for their identity cards. I felt angry with them as well as myself, particularly for their complacency. I toyed with the idea of catching them off guard and driving off — but I was also curious about who might want to see me so urgently. I did not have to wait long to find out; the man who greeted me effusively was short and barrel-chested, unmistakably Alexander Forbes.

"Thank you for coming, Mr Coll."

"Don't mention it. I'm always interested in widening my social circle."

He chuckled indulgently and dismissed my companions. The room was furnished lavishly but with little evidence of his own personality, and I wondered if it had been done for him professionally. One corner was dominated by a huge leather and chrome bar which looked as though it had been shipped from one of the night-clubs he owned. He gestured towards the enormous range of drinks on show. "Help yourself — I'll have a tomato juice."

After my recent experience I took no chances and uncapped two bottles of tomato juice, adding a few cubes of ice to the glasses.

As he accepted his drink I noticed how accustomed Forbes was to being waited on. He waved me to a seat. "I'll come straight to the point. I wanted to talk to you about our mutual friend, John Tarrant."

"The *late* John Tarrant?"

Surprisingly he went through the mourning ritual. "Terrible thing — man cut down in the prime of his life."

"Terrible," I agreed. "I didn't know you were friends?"

He nodded solemnly. "Several years. He printed two of my magazines."

Bloody stupid of me not to have checked on Tarrant's customers, I thought. "Versatile chap," I remarked. "Seems to have turned his hand to a variety of extramural activities. Did *you* share in any of them, Mr Forbes?"

"Such as what?"

I shrugged. "It's not for me to say. We hardly know each other so I don't want to cause offence, but the sort of things he dabbled in were — murder, forgery — printing banknotes too, I suspect."

Forbes nodded sagely. "Versatile, as you say. I don't like to speak ill of the dead, but the trouble with befriending men like that is that inevitably some of the dirt rubs off on one. I'll tell you frankly, Mr Coll, the Tarrant business is an embarrassment to me. I have enough enemies without rumours circulating about my relationship with him."

184

"Which was *what?*"

He studied me seriously for several seconds and then appeared to reach an important decision. "Mr Coll, I'm going to trust you."

I inclined my head graciously. "Be my guest."

He did not seem to notice my sarcasm, and continued. "John was a good printer. I respect good work. It transpired that we had a common interest in books. He was very knowledgeable, as you may know; he had an admirable collection." He paused to reflect for a moment. "I wonder what will happen to the books?"

"Perhaps, as two of his dearest surviving friends, we might put in a claim," I interjected, and this time he smiled.

"I must show you some of *my* books before you leave. Collection not as big as John's, but more selective."

"Got any original documents or letters of this Restoration period?"

He appeared not to hear, and returned to his story. "Which brings me to the journal you bought at Chestertons. John came up with an idea that was so ingenious that I was lost in admiration for him. Naturally I did not want to get involved in anything dishonest, but because I admired his audacity I agreed to put up a little money for his researches — what we might call the trial-and-error stage."

"For a small percentage?"

He flashed a look of indignation. "Naturally. But to me it did not represent a business venture so much as a lark. We didn't really expect the project to get off the ground."

"So your interest was philanthropic?"

There was suspicion in his eyes, but he did not rise

to the bait. "It doesn't matter now. What I am trying to say is that John Tarrant, God rest his soul, turned out to be something of a mad genius. I had nothing to do with the forgery; I was merely a friend in the background, but now I am in danger of being tarred with the same brush. I had no idea what I was getting into."

"You mean that he was a killer?"

"No idea," he repeated. "The first time I heard about the Dutchman's death was what I read in the paper. The connection didn't occur to me at first, but then I learned that John had been to Belgium for some print conference, and put two and two together. Seems he hired a car and drove across the border and back without anyone realising he had gone."

"Did he give you a reason?" I asked.

"Saw himself as a man of action. Others may have thought of forgery, but he actually did it. Same with getting rid of someone. Van der Meeren had demanded a large percentage of the sale price. John told him the facts of life — that the actual sale price had little bearing on the profit element, with all the costs involved. Mind you, although I wasn't part of the operation I agreed with John in saying that the Dutchman received a fair share for doing nothing, except get a little publicity. But it seems he wouldn't take no for an answer, and John killed him."

"How did you rope in van der Meeren at the start?"

Forbes appeared to stiffen with pride at the memory, although he managed to keep a poker-face. "What you might call original research. We needed a family who could possibly have known the Laniers and somehow get hold of her possessions on her death. Emilia had mixed a lot with musicians, particularly from Europe, a class that would have suffered severely when the Puritans came to power. Quite a few became destitute and returned to their own countries, to Italy, France and Holland. For a number of reasons, Holland was the easiest for our purpose, and after a few enquiries we found an historical society made up of descendants of people from the arts who left England before the Restoration. Some returned to England when Charles II came to the throne, so that reduced the numbers considerably."

"Impressive," I admitted.

He smiled. "It was. We ended up with three individuals who had no living relatives to complicate the issue. One was a clergyman it was thought safer not to proposition; another lived in a high-rise block, the type who wouldn't know what to do with an old journal, apart from starting a fire with it — which left van der Meeren, who was most accommodating."

It was significant that for the first time Forbes had used the term 'we', and not attributed the entire operation to Tarrant. I wondered how much of the story was true, but was not bothered; it was the first full account of what might have happened — whoever had been the true leader.

"What part did Charlotte Hesse play in all this?" I asked.

He smiled affectionately at the mention of her name. "None. John said that you had a bee in your bonnet about her, but it was not in his interests to put you right. The more attention you paid to Charlotte, the less you were likely to bother with him."

I told him why I had suspected her, and he nodded in agreement. "Very logical. Don't worry about it; no damage has been done. As a matter of fact, the one thing for which I have to thank John was introducing me to Charlotte. He wasn't very happy later when he found out I had replaced him in the lady's affections, but he was realistic about it — after all, we were not being frivolous. I'm very fond of the lady."

I asked if I could have another drink. With less cause for suspicion now I helped myself to a whisky and ice. Standing by the bar I toasted his good health, and added, "That was all very interesting, but I'm sure you didn't bring me here for a heart-to-heart. You must want something from me in return?"

"Naturally. I'm sure there's nothing for me to worry about, especially now the journal has disappeared, but I prefer to err on the side of caution."

"Disappeared?" I echoed. "What are you talking about?"

"Didn't you know? I would have thought someone would have told you."

"*You* tell me," I urged.

He shrugged. "All I know is what I read the other day in one of the papers; a few lines saying that burglars had made off with the Lanier manuscript which had recently been bought at a London auction. The report described it as one of the most daring raids ever carried out at an American university. I'm sure I can lay my hands on a copy if you don't believe me."

I was shaken by the news, but even in my shocked state experienced a pang of sympathy for Tom Duncan who had loved his prize possession so passionately. We had had our differences, but the theft of his 'baby' swept aside such petty wrangles. How ironic that after our argument, and my obsession with laboratory tests, the manuscript had been snatched from us? Surely, in hindsight, even a forged journal was better than none. "Do they know who the burglars are?" I asked.

He shook his head. "It was only a four- or five-line report."

"So it's turned out very well for you in the circumstances?" I pointed out.

"I don't know the legal position. Didn't they once bring a ship's steward to trial for murdering a woman passenger, even though her body was never found? In any case, I'm more worried about my reputation. As far as I know there's nothing in John's papers to link me with his forgery. In fact, the only person who keeps harping on it — is you."

I smiled. "It hasn't made me very popular."

"Frankly, I can't see what the fuss is about. What does it matter? At the moment everyone is blissfully ignorant, including the thieves. As a bookseller you know that a manuscript — *any* manuscript — is worth what someone is prepared to pay for it. Some of the Thomas Wise forgeries, for example, are worth more today than the first editions he copied."

"That's true," I conceded. "But we do have a *choice*, being in possession of the facts. If my customer had known the truth and didn't care, then who am I to argue? But meanwhile, it's my duty to present them with the *facts*."

He nodded. "I can understand that. I don't agree, but I respect you for it. My suggestion is this: *we* know that John Tarrant was responsible for the forgery and the murder. Why don't you — seeing that you seem to see yourself as Don Quixote — prepare a statement setting out the facts as we see them. It would put your customer in the picture, and satisfy the police if they even care."

189

"I intended to do something like that." I was stalling for time to think, because I wondered whether telling Tom Duncan the truth now might not be twisting the knife in the wound — apart from preventing the library from getting their insurance pay-out.

Not knowing what was going on in my mind, Forbes was becoming complacent. "On further consideration," he said, thinking aloud, "we might even forget about the police at this stage. It would be more effective if they found out about it later from an independent source if needs be. All *I* ask is that you don't bring in side issues, such as my very tenuous link with John."

I knew what I was going to do, and I could have lied to him, but my conscience rebelled at his smugness. "I can't do that, Mr Forbes."

He looked surprised and hurt. "Why on earth not? I'm not asking you to lie. I'm suggesting you stick to the main facts, and not stray off at tangents."

"I understand that; it wouldn't have worried me if the story had ended there, but you've forgotten that someone killed Tarrant, *and* tried to frame me. I can't turn a blind eye to that."

"You don't think *I* had . . ."

I interrupted impatiently. "You probably killed van der Meeren too."

He joined me at the bar, but it was not to get a drink. On the wall behind, next to the light-switch, was a white button which he pressed. Within ten seconds my 'CID' men came in; they barely glanced at me, remaining relaxed but alert by the door.

"I don't know how strong your principles are when it comes to people getting hurt," Forbes continued smoothly, as though he had barely noticed

190

them.

"I'm not frightened of your thugs, Mr Forbes. I may only be able to call on one and a half hands, but I can still take care of them."

"Don't overlook me!" he said mildly. "I'm not young any more and I prefer to pay others — *specialists* — for this sort of thing, but I'm still pretty fit." He stopped for effect, and I could see that he was well able to look after himself. Trying to cope with three of them was not a pleasant prospect. Then he smiled as though he was trying to repair a silly misunderstanding between friends. "In any case, you misunderstood my question. I was not threatening *you*. What is your telephone number?"

I told him and he used the telephone on the bar to dial Ardley. He let it ring three times before deliberately disconnecting the line and trying again. This time it was answered by a voice he expected. I was disconcerted; it was not Charlie Appleton's voice.

Forbes anticipated my reaction. "I understand you're very fond of Mr Appleton. Nice old man, it's said; never did anyone any harm."

My heart sank. Charlie was staying at the house in my absence to save the daily journey from his home twenty miles away. Forbes handed me the phone. My voice was unsteady. "Hello?"

After a momentary pause Charlie's voice came on the line, loudly with the awkwardness of elderly people still distrustful of the phone. "Don't worry about me, Matt," he said defiantly. "I'll be all right."

But I *was* worried. "What happened, Charlie?"

I heard the phone being snatched away from him, and a younger voice took over. "He won't get hurt if you do as you're told. We're just sitting here

191

playing cards."

I turned to Forbes who reached over and replaced the receiver. "You can believe that, Mr Coll. Nobody likes hurting old men, but if it should be necessary . . . My man will stay down there until you've obliged me. There are five hours difference between us and the Eastern seaboard of the States, so there's no reason why you shouldn't *phone* your customer now. Tell them what we've agreed, and say you'll put a letter of confirmation in the post."

"There's no point — the librarian is not there; he's on a buying tour of Europe."

"That's right, but you can speak to his deputy. I can't rely on a letter because it takes several days, and in the interim you might have a change of heart. Once this is sorted out we can all relax."

"There is still Tarrant's murder to explain away."

He was indifferent. "There's nothing to connect me or any of my friends with that. It could have been anyone, including that bitch of a wife he hated so much."

Although I was not prepared to jeopardise Charlie's safety I estimated it was worth one 'hit-or-miss' attempt at overpowering them. If I lost I would do as they asked. My only chance was to catch them off guard, so I stalled, appearing to give in to their demands but arguing over the terms. "How do I know you'll keep your word?"

Forbes was standing with his back to the bar about two or three feet to my right, and his men faced us across the room about twelve feet away. Before I finished the sentence, still looking straight ahead, I chopped the hard bottom edge of my right hand in a backward arc against the bridge of his nose. I relied on memory but the scything action was spot

192

on, and even as he grunted with pain I suspected I had broken the bone. Without stopping to admire my handiwork, I grabbed the soda-siphon off the bar.

The terrible twins, as I was beginning to think of them, separated so that they could come at me from different angles; their advance cautious, not bothered by the loss of Forbes whom they had obviously dismissed as an amateur in these matters, despite his pride. I was saving the makeshift weapon until I could see the whites of their eyes, so there was time to glance at Forbes. He was pressing a handkerchief to his nose, and I could see that when he had recovered from the initial shock that pride would make him come at me again, so I swivelled my left leg round to kick him in the groin. From that moment he would want nothing but the haven of unconsciousness for the next hour or so.

Forbes' men were now no more than 5 feet away, and I was particularly conscious of blue blazer menacing my vulnerable left side. At point-blank range I hurled the soda siphon at his head. It was heavy enough to have knocked him out, but his reactions were lightning fast and he ducked underneath. Instinctively, or perhaps it was desperation, I kicked at his bobbing head and caught him on the chest; a blow hard enough to knock him back on his haunches. The man in brown, taking advantage of my exposed right side leapt in to close with me. From his pocket he had produced a black-jack, and by raising his hand to smash the weight down on my head, he gave me a split second escape-route. I squatted down and pushed my shoulders against his knees so that he overbalanced. But now I was on the ground, and his companion dived on top of me. I struggled to shake him off, but his partner returned and got in a kick that nearly took off one of my ears.

The ringing in my head was now joined by what sounded like the ringing of a doorbell. I concentrated and heard hammering and shouting below. "Police: open up!" Despite the pain in my ear I felt like cheering, although blue blazer refused to let go of me.

Then there was a shattering noise downstairs as a door at the back was broken down. One of the terrible twins hurried over to his employer and tried to get some sense out of him, but Forbes was too befuddled with pain. He came back, and the two 'bodyguards' stood over me indecisively while they debated the options. They had not got very far when the door was thrust open, and in charged two uniformed and two plain-clothes policemen. The cavalry had arrived as tradition demands in the nick of time.

ELEVEN

I owed my rescue to Charlotte Hesse. My disclosure that the Herbert letter was stolen had alarmed her. She recalled that although she had been unsuspecting at the time, Forbes had manipulated the proposed sale so that, either way, the letter would be offered exclusively to me; how, too, he had made her withdraw the letter as soon as the results of the laboratory tests were known. She had accepted the argument that he had always maintained a low profile in connection with his hobby, and that would now be impossible, but Jonathon Harker had been displeased and even suspicious of the apparent change of heart after all the bother and inconvenience to which he had been put. She had intended to demand an explanation, and in normal circumstances would have waited until they met or spoke in the ordinary way. She was, after all, still in love with Forbes and might, or might not, have accepted his answers. But when she glanced out of the window to watch me leave, she recognised one of the men who accosted me. In that split second Charlotte realised there was a connection between the Herbert letter and the Lanier forgery, and another between them and Tarrant's death — that it could only have been Forbes who had arranged the murder, and that the same fate might be in store for me. There was no time for reflection; she had dialled 999.

All this I discovered later at Laura's flat when we took the opportunity to apologise for our conduct. Fortunately, the rapport that had developed between the women was strong enough to survive the embarrassment, and when I explained my own reasons to Charlotte I suspect she may have been secretly flattered that she had been credited with such talent and ingenuity.

Yet although I said nothing to them, I was not completely satisfied we had really got to the bottom of the mystery. Something that Forbes had said worried me. I checked in my diary for the date of the 15th International Book Fair, held that year in Holland, and found that it was due to open in two days' time. I telephoned Inspector Heemskerk in Amsterdam and asked for his co-operation.

The fair, as the name suggests, brought together the top antiquarian booksellers in Europe, and the standard of books on display was a cut above what I would normally expect to sell in the shop. For this reason it was my first visit — Amsterdam is an expensive place if one is merely coming to browse — but I had other reasons for attending now. The exhibition was housed in the main banqueting-suite on the ground floor of the 25-storey Van Gogh hotel; there were nearly a hundred stands representing seven countries.

The hotel was fully booked, so I stayed at the Europa again, arriving at the Fair in good time for the opening ceremony. I enjoyed myself for the first hour or so wandering about the show like a normal visitor. As it happened, it was also a frustrating experience, and I cursed myself for not bringing a cheque-book, since a number of items were far less expensive than I had imagined. I saw several friends and acquaintances among the British visitors and exhibitors before bumping into Tom Duncan, although it was he who spotted me first.

"Final fling before going back to work?" I joked. His grin was half-hearted, and I wondered if the rather subdued manner was something to do with the burglary. I extended my sympathies and asked if there was any news or developments.

He shook his head. "It's early days, although the cops were not too optimistic."

"Did they take anything else?"

"You're kidding? Those guys were pros; they took the cream of our manuscript collection. Individually there was nothing as valuable as the Lanier — nor anything, between you and me, of such *sentimental* value — but it was a pretty substantial haul."

"You *were* insured?"

"You should know that money can't replace that sort of material. Manuscripts are unique."

"Of course, but at least you can go on a spending-spree. Without wishing to sound unfeeling, you're bound to find *something* to console you."

He laughed. "I don't even have that satisfaction. My deputy or my replacement, if Frank doesn't get the position, will have that privilege. I finally decided to accept one of the plush jobs I pretended to look down on. It's not so much what they offered me, but the size of the acquisitions budget I'll be handling — ten times what I have been used to."

"Which is the lucky university?"

197

He whispered in my ear; I whistled. Tom Duncan had made it. I wondered inconsequentially whether he would still use me to represent him at auctions, or whether he would now consider it was more appropriate to work with major firms like Frensham's. And as though he had telepathic powers, Wilfred Frensham suddenly appeared at my side and greeted us. He and Duncan knew each other, so I excused myself and announced that I was going to look at some other exhibits. In fact, I moved to the end of the long room, glanced back to ensure that they were engrossed in their conversation, and slipped out into the lobby.

Inspector Heemskerk was standing by the reception-desk, and we exchanged nods before I took the lift to the fifth floor. About half-way up I heard the fire-alarm bell start to ring, making me jump despite the fact it was expected. I imagined the scene in the exhibition area, with Heemskerk or someone in authority appealing for calm as they announced the evacuation of the hotel, and asking visitors and exhibitors to file into the courtyard, away from the main hotel. "Everything is under control, but you are requested *not* to go upstairs for the time being," being the gist of the instruction, and it was for someone who was prepared to defy that warning that I was now lying in wait, standing just inside the door of the fifth-floor men's toilet. The place seemed deserted, but I opened the door a crack and listened for footsteps. I did not have to wait long.

When the sound had passed I looked out — and saw Tom Duncan. Outside his room he looked both ways before going in, but he did not see me. I followed, standing in the open doorway as he searched for

198

something that should have been in a suitcase. When he did not find it, Duncan refused to panic, sitting down on one of the twin beds while he tried to fathom out whether his memory was playing tricks on him. Eventually he became aware of my presence and remarked without looking round: "We're supposed to be in the courtyard downstairs. I came up for my passport and a few personal papers — just in case the hotel burns to the ground." He tried a laugh, but it was a weak effort.

I nodded. "Why don't I help? Four eyes are better than two."

He got up agitatedly and came to the door to push me out. "Don't be a damn fool, Matt. There's a fire somewhere in the building — we don't want to risk being *trapped* up here!"

I switched to my cool expression. "They said it was under control. In any case, I heard it was on the *sixth* floor, so we should at least have time to find your passport."

"You don't understand, I seem to have *mislaid* it."

I approached the wardrobe. "I'll help."

"For Chrissake, mind your own damn business!" He grabbed my arm and pulled me towards the door. The fire-bell stopped ringing, and he relaxed momentarily so that I was able to evade his grip and go back. "I think I can see it," I announced, dropping to my knees and looking under the bed.

"Are you mad?" he demanded. "There's nothing under there!"

I produced a slim black leather overnight-case with the initials "T.D." and held it up for his inspection. "*Voila.*"

"Oh!" he said, stunned by what I had just found.

199

"Thanks." He stretched out a hand, but I beat him to it and opened the case. Inside was the Lanier journal. I decided not to add insult to injury with any comment.

Tom Duncan sat down on the bed; he said nothing at first, but I could see that even now he was searching for a way out. "Is the panic over?" he eventually asked.

I nodded. "You should have done as you were advised and gone into the courtyard."

Heemskerk came into the room, and visibly relaxed when he saw the journal. He had not been enthusiastic about the deception, but as I had anticipated he was ambitious enough to consider the end justified the means — and my preliminary briefing had satisfied him that the plan was likely to work. I introduced them formally.

"I am an American citizen," Duncan warned him. "Before we go any further I insist on seeing somebody from my Embassy."

"Before we go any further, Mr Duncan? *Where*, further?"

Duncan sneered. "You can't intimidate me — I'm not one of your long-haired, left-wing students. I don't know what you're trying to prove, but you've probably been conned by Matt here. He's got an obsession about the journal."

"Not surprising, considering the criminal activity it seems to generate," Heemskerk remarked mildly. "I believe that journal is what you would call 'hot'?"

"All I know is that I was in Germany when the journal was stolen; you can check that. I hadn't seen it in weeks — until just now — when it was planted on me. You've only got his word that he found it in my case."

Heemskerk nodded gravely. "Of course."

"Did you know he set off the hotel fire-alarm? Or was it you? The authorities certainly won't give either of you a pat on the back! It could have caused a panic — people could have been killed."

Heemskerk acknowledged the point. "Your consideration does you credit, Mr Duncan, but to set your mind at rest I can assure you that periodic fire-drill is a statutory regulation, and the hotel management and I merely agreed to combine our interests. At this time of day practically all of the upstairs rooms are unoccupied, and the exhibition area is virtually a separate unit. If you remember, when I made the announcement I did not say there was a fire; merely asked people in the exhibition area to proceed to the courtyard. Members of the public in other parts of the hotel were told that it was an exercise."

"We needed to get into your room," I interrupted. "You were unlikely to admit the Lanier was in your possession, and in deference to Inspector Heemskerk I didn't want to break in."

"So what have you proved?" Duncan said defiantly. "I told you I was out of the country when the burglary took place. How it got into my case is a mystery — unless you put it there."

"I am not interested in your burglary, Mr Duncan," said Heemskerk. "Naturally if you have a statement to make I will be happy to convey it to my colleagues in your country, but meanwhile I am more concerned with the murder of a Dutch citizen, Dr van der Meeren. I believe you can help us with our enquiries."

This time Duncan was shaken. "Murder? You're crazy — I've never heard of the guy."

"Come off it, Tom," I interrupted in exasperation. "It was his death that first planted the germ of the idea the journal could be a forgery."

"Are you still on about that?" he said.

"I'm afraid you've been overtaken by events. Tarrant confessed his part — before he died."

"Died?"

"It was murder," I pointed out. "But fortunately he had already given us the full story."

"You're bluffing."

I was, but dared not admit it, and continued in the same vein. "We knew Tarrant was connected with van der Meeren's death, and since you were one of his partners, Inspector Heemskerk naturally wanted to interview you — after which the English police will want to know about your part in *Tarrant's* murder."

Duncan was beginning to sweat, but his protest had all the spontaneous indignation of truth. "I haven't been in Great Britain for a couple of weeks."

"It has to be you," I bluffed, "because of motive. The only other person with a similar one is Alexander Forbes, and he denies it too." He groaned at Forbes' name, obviously shocked that we knew all about both confederates, and I set out to consolidate my position. "Look Tom, *I* don't think you killed Tarrant, but when it comes down to it, it will be your word against that of Forbes — and he has very powerful friends in my country. You don't imagine he would think twice about double-crossing *you*?"

"I've nothing to say," he replied.

"How do you think I got on to you?" I demanded. "At first Forbes tried to put all the blame on Tarrant, no longer around to defend himself. He did concede that he had put up some cash for Tarrant's experi-

202

mental work, but tried to kid me it was little more than a philanthropic gesture — so it meant that *he* was in it up to the hilt, too. At that stage your name had not cropped up at all, and when Forbes mentioned the burglary he claimed he only knew what he had read in the paper — the bare outline. That was where he slipped up, because a moment later when I volunteered the fact you were in Europe, he said he *knew*! He and Tarrant might have been crooks, but neither had the in-depth knowledge of Emilia, her background or even the period."

"If you're pointing that finger at me," Duncan said, "I can't deny I had the knowledge, but what motive could I have?"

"I can think of one."

"Oh? I'd like to hear it?"

"My hunch is that you did it for *yourself*. First, possibly, there was the supreme satisfaction of knowing you had outsmarted the world — at least, the world that matters to you. Second, would have been the *prestige* of being able to acquire something unique that would be envied by your peers. It was a situation where *you* couldn't lose; even if my bid had not been successful there would have still been the 'consolation' of sharing the financial rewards."

Duncan grinned. "Where's your proof?"

I pointed to the journal on the bed. "That. You couldn't bear to let it go."

"We are wasting time," interjected Heemskerk. "My only interest is the murder of van der Meeren, and you are a prime suspect. Telling us the truth about your rôle in the conspiracy is the only way you can hope to clear yourself of the more serious charge."

Duncan nodded his agreement. "Matt wasn't far

out when he talked about the prestige. It was probably on the strength of me winning the manuscript in the face of all that competition that did more than anything to clinch the job I've just accepted. You see, the timing of its appearance at auction was crucial. With all due respect to Matt who did his job well enough we had to narrow the odds. If you care to think back you'll find that we delayed its appearance until after the big sales in London and New York in the previous three months — where most of my rivals spent the bulk of their budgets not knowing our journal even existed. That was what counted. You should know by now that *money* isn't that important to me; nor the satisfaction you guessed at. I didn't need any evidence that I could outsmart them — I already knew."

"I should have thought of it before — when Inspector Heemskerk admitted he had entertained suspicions of *me*," I said, "although he was thinking about the financial gain. It had to be someone on the inside, and there were so few of us."

"I had nothing to do with any murder," Duncan retorted. "I'll give you the facts and you can check them out." He switched his attention to the Inspector. "It seems the days of the talented individual in crime are numbered — we've been replaced by organised crime. And yet the individual can still score if he can go it alone. As soon as he has to rely on others, the odds are stacked against him."

"But you *needed* help with something of that scale," I pointed out.

He shook his head. "If I had taken as much care in choosing my partners as I did in the writing — if I had not grabbed at what seemed a good opportunity, I wouldn't be talking to you like this today. Tarrant

204

was a craftsman, but he was also a head case, and I would have spotted that in time.

"It all started with Alexander. He comes to the States regularly, and I got to know him through friends; he's an impressive guy, and we had this common interest in books. I don't even remember who actually raised the subject of forgery — it doesn't really matter — but we had a stimulating discussion about the morality, the technicalities, and the challenge. I remember that in a whole series of hypothetical situations his observations were so perceptive — I was still thinking about them long after we had parted.

"I came up with the germ of an idea, and eventually when I sounded him out he agreed to help, at least to put up some cash to do a feasibility study. He told me he had a printer who was also a bibliophile and could probably get the paper, and fix the binding, if I could fabricate the diary and actually write the material."

"So the theory that it had to have been written by a woman was another of your red herrings?" I asked.

Duncan laughed. "It turned out to be a labour of love. At the outset we intended to cheat, to knock out a few pages, and then upset ink over the remainder 'as though she had started the journal and never finished. But when I got into the head of Emilia I felt a compulsion to keep going. I felt I *was* her."

I acknowledged the validity of that remark. "It must have been a weird experience later when two or three of us became quite infatuated with her?"

"It was a combination of pride — and embarrass-ment. After all, I had spent nearly six months just

205

working out her thought-processes before even putting pen to paper, and in all that time we were prepared to cut our losses. And, as I said, it would have worked out if we had not employed a schizophrenic like Tarrant. Van der Meeren could have been handled with more sublety."

"Forbes told me that part of it," I interjected.

"And also I suppose that Tom Duncan lost patience with Tarrant and got rid of him? I *swear* I know nothing about that!"

"What about the burglary?" asked Heemskerk.

"We decided — Forbes and me — that the journal had become a liability. It had served its purpose, and despite my efforts to reassure Matt, he was still making us nervous. Sooner or later we might have had to get those lab tests carried out. Anyway, the university research team had practically finished its work." He broke off and looked at me triumphantly. "Did you know the university's publishing operation were talking of issuing a *facsimile* edition for general sale at $15?"

I shook my head, but he could see I was impressed, and continued: "Forbes has contacts with certain people I would rather not know about, and with a little help from me about general security and the alarm system in particular they did what had to be done."

"Didn't your conscience trouble you at all?"

He shrugged. "I love that library. Several years of my life have gone into making it what it is today. But it was necessary, and if anything we were *over*-insured, so the money can be put to good use — while I make a fresh start."

"What happened to the manuscripts they stole?" demanded Heemskerk.

"Forbes will keep them under wraps for the time being."

"And the Lanier?"

He grimaced. "At least I can't blame him for *that*. I asked for the journal, and he handed it over when I was in London – in fact a couple of days after I came to see you. You were right. It was sentimentality on my part – couldn't bear to let it go." He appeared to reflect on the situation for a moment, and his caution reasserted itself. "Hey, I agreed to tell you about the forgery – not the burglary. What about doing a deal?"

He looked at me, and I passed the buck to Heemskerk, but the Dutchman shook his head. "I am not a judge, Mr Duncan; merely a gatherer of information. The decision rests with the police on the spot."

"I shall deny everything," Duncan said.

Heemskerk shrugged indifferently; it was not his problem. Suddenly I experienced a sneaking sympathy for the librarian. "Why don't you stay in Europe and make a fresh start?"

He swallowed with difficulty. "God, I had forgotten about the *library* authorities! They don't need *proof*; the merest glimpse of a police uniform on the campus and I would be *out*."

"So resign first and stay in Europe!"

He did not seem to hear me. "I set out to be Number One, and I *made* it. How the mighty hath fallen."

I could see that he would never be content to work in some backwater, or as the assistant to another librarian. Even leaving the library service was surely preferable to that type of subordination. But I had forgotten that Duncan still had another option. He snatched the journal from the bed and hurled it in

207

our direction, using the split second distraction to move towards the window. For a moment I thought we could reach him as he passed to open it — but the hotel windows were sealed to accommodate the air-conditioning. Even as that realisation dawned, Heemskerk and I were stunned by the sudden explosion of noise as the glass shattered. We seemed to freeze in another dimension as Duncan projected himself into space. It was his disappearance that brought us back to the present, and we reached the gaping hole simultaneously.

Five floors below Duncan was sprawled face down on the pavement, pedestrians beginning to form an uneasy circle around him. Heemskerk used the phone to call an ambulance, but we suspected it was a formality. In the group below someone was feeling Duncan's pulse, but from the lack of urgency in the manner it also seemed a token gesture.

Heemskerk went out, and I was about to follow, but stopped at the journal, face down and hinges straining, on the floor. Instinctively I picked it up, concerned to see any book treated with such inconsideration. In closing the covers I could not resist glancing at the last page. Concluding a rambling passage of complaint about her misfortunes was Emilia's final sentence. " . . . I pray the man who abewses me or shal profit from my name shal bee cast downe to Hell."

Shutting the journal for the last time, and looking down at the cluster of people in the street, I wondered if as he crashed through the glass Tom Duncan had recalled his prophetic last words — his legacy of the Dark Lady.